Sixteen Hou[...] Course Across [...] Ocean, When Ea[...] The Other…Interesting.

Sixteen hours, Sara marveled, unable to look away from Mr. Cordello's gaze. Sara was going to be trapped in extremely close confines with this *extremely interesting* man for sixteen hours.

Of course, they wouldn't be alone during that time, she reminded herself. There would be two pilots and two flight attendants aboard, as well. And the crew's presence would go a long way toward keeping her in line and preventing her from doing anything rash. Something like, oh, say…leaping across the aisle and straddling Mr. Cordello's waist and covering his mouth with her own and kissing him and kissing him and…

Where was she? Oh, yes. Sixteen hours. Right. It was a rather long time to be saddling—or rather, saddled *with,* she hastily corrected herself—the man.

Sixteen hours. They were in for an *interesting* trip!

* * *

Don't miss the exciting conclusion to the **Crown and Glory** series next month with **ROYALLY PREGNANT by Barbara McCauley** (SD #1480).

Dear Reader,

Wondering what to put on your holiday wish list? How about six passionate, powerful and provocative new love stories from Silhouette Desire!

This month, bestselling author Barbara Boswell returns to Desire with our MAN OF THE MONTH, SD #1471, *All in the Game*, featuring a TV reality-show contestant who rekindles an off-screen romance with the chief cameraman while her identical twin wonders what's going on.

In SD #1472, *Expecting…and In Danger* by Eileen Wilks, a Connelly hero tries to protect and win the trust of a secretive, pregnant lover. It's the latest episode in the DYNASTIES: THE CONNELLYS series—the saga of a wealthy Chicago-based clan.

A desert prince loses his heart to a feisty intern in SD #1473, *Delaney's Desert Sheikh* by award-winning author Brenda Jackson. This title marks Jackson's debut as a Desire author. In SD #1474, *Taming the Prince* by Elizabeth Bevarly, a blue-collar bachelor trades his hard hat for a crown…and a wedding ring? This is the second Desire installment in the exciting CROWN AND GLORY series.

Matchmaking relatives unite an unlikely couple in SD #1475, *A Lawman in Her Stocking* by Kathie DeNosky. And SD #1476, *Do You Take This Enemy?* by reader favorite Sara Orwig, is a marriage-of-convenience story featuring a pregnant heroine whose groom is from a feuding family. This title is the first in Orwig's compelling STALLION PASS miniseries.

Make sure you get all six of Silhouette Desire's hot November romances.

Enjoy!

Joan Marlow Golan

Joan Marlow Golan
Senior Editor, Silhouette Desire

Please address questions and book requests to:
Silhouette Reader Service
U.S.: 3010 Walden Ave., P.O. Box 1325, Buffalo, NY 14269
Canadian: P.O. Box 609, Fort Erie, Ont. L2A 5X3

Taming the Prince

ELIZABETH BEVARLY

Published by Silhouette Books
America's Publisher of Contemporary Romance

Special thanks and acknowledgment are given to
Elizabeth Bevarly for her contribution to
the CROWN AND GLORY series.

 SILHOUETTE BOOKS

ISBN 0-373-76474-X

TAMING THE PRINCE

Copyright © 2002 by Harlequin Books S.A.

Visit Silhouette at www.eHarlequin.com

Printed in U.S.A.

ELIZABETH BEVARLY

was born and raised in Louisville, Kentucky, and earned her B.A. with honors in English from the University of Louisville in 1983. Although she never wanted to be anything but a novelist, her career side trips before making the leap to writing included stints working in movie theaters, restaurants, boutiques and a major department store. She also spent time as an editorial assistant for a medical journal, where she learned the correct spelling and meanings of a variety of words (such as *microscopy* and *histological*) that she will never, ever use again. When she's not writing, Elizabeth enjoys old movies, old houses, good books, whimsical antiques, hot jazz and even hotter salsa (the music, not the sauce). She has claimed as residences Washington, D.C., northern Virginia, southern New Jersey and Puerto Rico, but she now resides with her husband and young son back home in Kentucky, where she fully intends to remain.

For David. You *are* my prince.

One

It didn't take a lot to make Shane Cordello happy. Just a flawless blue sky overhead, a balmy Southern California breeze ruffling his hair, the spicy aroma of kielbasa and onions on the grill, and the rhythmic, incessant *bam-bam-bam-bam* of a diligent jackhammer as it pulverized the pavement nearby.

Yeah, life didn't get any better than that.

Which meant that today was an ideal day for Shane. After punching the time clock at the construction site where he worked as foreman, he headed to the lunch wagon parked just beyond the gate for one of those savory kielbasas. He skimmed off his battered hard hat as he went, running his fingers briskly through his sweat-dampened, shaggy brown hair.

The front of his denim work shirt was damp, too, he noted as he loosened the obligatory necktie that his position as foreman dictated he wear—though not on his off-hours, and lunch hour was one of those, by God—as were the

knees of his faded blue jeans, though that last was due not
to perspiration, but to the fact that he'd had to kneel down
in the mud to look for the gold Waterman pen his mother
had given him for his twenty-third birthday earlier in the
year. When he'd finally found it, he'd taken it back to the
foreman's trailer and tucked it into his desk where he intended to leave it. He wasn't the kind of man who should
be responsible for things like solid gold pens. He was much
better suited to clicking a plastic—disposable—Bic.

Yeah, disposable was the way to keep it, Shane thought.
It didn't pay to get too attached to material things in life,
because they'd only get taken away from you, sooner or
later, one way or another. He'd learned that, if not much
else, during his sojourn on the planet.

He squinted his blue eyes against the sun beating down
on him as he made his way toward the lunch wagon. November didn't bring a cold autumn to L.A. the way it did
to other parts of the country, but the air was definitely a
bit cooler today and felt a bit less sunbaked than it had
during the summer months. It was the ocean more than the
air that signified the change of seasons in Southern California. These days, Shane was wearing his wet suit all the
time when he surfed, because the temperature of the water
had plummeted since summer—and even then, it had been
none too warm. Other than having to don his wet suit on
the weekends now, though, he hadn't seen any big changes
come into his life recently. Nor was he anticipating any to
come anytime soon.

And that, of course, was just the way he liked it.

Amy Collins, who ran the lunch wagon that had visited
the construction site daily since work had begun a week
earlier, smiled when she saw Shane coming, anticipating
his desire—his lunch desire, anyway—by forking up a kielbasa loaded with onions before he even asked for one. As
for his other desires…

Well, it was no secret to anyone on the Wellman Towers
site that Amy had been trying since day one to capture

Shane's interest. And, truth be told, he wasn't completely immune to her charms. She was darkly pretty, round in all the right places, boisterously outspoken, even downright sassy at times, which was just the way he normally liked his women. But there was something about Amy, too, that told Shane she played for keeps when it came to men. And *keeps* was a place he never wanted to find himself, especially with a woman. Mainly because he knew too well that *keeps* didn't exist—not in his little corner of the world, anyway. So he steered clear of Amy, knowing she'd meet a forever-after kind of guy someday.

Just, you know, not today.

"Hey, Amy," he greeted her as he stopped in front of the window and dug into a denim pocket for a few wadded-up dollar bills.

"Hel-lo, Shane," she replied in a soft, singsongy kind of purr.

He smiled in response, not necessarily because he liked her purr all that much—in fact, he found it kind of off-putting, truth be told—but because he always responded to women with a smile. Shane liked women. All women. A lot. And women seemed to like him, too. All women. A lot. So it was only natural that he greeted one with a smile whenever he met one. Even if she did purr.

"How's it going?" he asked. The question was, at best, mechanical, at worst, hypothetical. Shane didn't really expect or require an answer.

But Amy replied anyway. "I could be better, actually," she said, smiling back. Her cheek dimpled with the action, a gesture he was somehow certain she'd spent years perfecting. "It's been kind of lonely this week. But there's a new Schwarzenegger movie opening up this weekend," she added, having heard Shane remark that he was a big fan of both the actor and action films. "Want to go with me on Friday?"

"I can't this Friday, Amy. Thanks, anyway."

"Saturday, then?" she asked audaciously without missing a beat.

He shook his head. "I can't this weekend at all. Stuff going on."

She expelled a breath that bordered on impatient, and her smile fell some. "Stuff going on," she echoed dubiously. "Right. You know, Shane, you could give a girl a complex, if you're not careful."

"Oh, I don't want to do that," he said honestly. "I really am going to be busy this weekend, Amy. That's all." There was no reason to tell her, he decided, that he was going to be busy doing nothing. That probably came under the heading of Too Much Knowledge.

"Yeah, right," she said, punctuating the comment with a *hmpf* for good measure. "I bet the queen of England herself has called you up to invite you to tea."

Shane grinned again and was about to offer some flip response when he was halted by the sound of his name sailing through the crisp afternoon air.

"Yo, Cordello!"

The voice bellowing the summons came loud and strong from the foreman's trailer, and when Shane turned in that direction, he saw Daniel Mendoza, the contractor for Wellman Towers—oh, yeah, and his boss, too—standing at the open door of the trailer. He was holding his hand beside his head, forefinger and pinky extended, in the internationally recognized hand gesture for "You've got a phone call, dude." Seeing it, though, immediately roused Shane's apprehension.

Who would be calling him at work? he wondered anxiously. Most of his friends were co-workers on this very site, and those who weren't knew better than to disturb him during the workday. His mother was currently honeymooning with husband number five in Tahiti—not that Shane thought the marriage would last much beyond the honeymoon, because they rarely did for her—so she was sure to have other things on her mind at the moment.

And his brother, Marcus, lived in Chicago and had way too much going on in his workaholic life to call Shane more than once or twice a month, and Shane had just spoken to him about a week ago. Not that Shane held it against his fraternal twin to be relatively incommunicado. Hell, his own life was plenty full these days, with work, if nothing else. He and Marcus had a solid, close relationship, one that transcended a need for constant communication. And that was no easy feat considering the fact that the two of them had been separated by divorce at nine years of age, when Shane went to live with their mother and Marcus went to live with their father. But the two boys had spent a month together every summer while they were growing up, and even in that limited amount of time, they'd managed to forge the kind of bond that few brothers—hell, few twins, for that matter—forged when they were raised in the same household.

Shane's father was someone he rarely saw or heard from these days, so long ago had the two of them lost touch, and he doubted the elder Cordello would be calling him for any reason, at work *or* at home. So since Shane's friends were all here on the site, and his relations were all hundreds of miles away with other things on their minds, then there was no reason for anyone to be calling him at work. Not unless…

Not unless it was an emergency.

Leaving the kielbasa sitting on the lunch wagon window where Amy had placed it, Shane sprinted toward the foreman's trailer with a sick feeling in the pit of his stomach. That sickness grew more resolute with each stride he completed, until it had coalesced into a cold, greasy lump when he saw the grim expression on his employer's face. Oh, no…

"What is it, Mr. Mendoza?" he asked breathlessly as he took the trailer's metal stairs two at a time.

His boss's expression turned malevolent. "I've told all

of you that personal phone calls to or from this site are prohibited.''

Shane relaxed at the censure. If Mr. Mendoza was this ticked off, the call couldn't be much of an emergency. "I'm sorry," Shane apologized, even though he'd had little control over who might have picked up a telephone and dialed this particular number. "Who is it?"

"A *woman*," his boss said with distaste, making clear his opinion of that half of the world's population.

Shane's earlier concern changed immediately to confusion. "A woman?" he repeated. "I've never given this number to any women." In fact, he hadn't given it to anyone but Marcus. With strict instructions that his brother only dial it in case of emergency, Shane couldn't help recalling, his anxiety rising to the fore once again. "What woman? What does she want?" he asked.

"How the hell should I know what woman?" Mr. Mendoza snapped. "She says it's *personal*," he added, his voice dripping with even more repugnance than before on that final word. Obviously the man disliked personal matters even more than he disliked women. "And she sounds like a woman who's old enough to be your mother. Frankly, Cordello, I do *not* want to go there. It's just too—" He punctuated the statement by giving his entire body a shudder of disgust.

Ignoring the other man, Shane's confusion turning again to concern, he snatched up the phone. "Mother?" he said without preamble. "What is it? What's wrong?"

There was a slight pause from the other end of the line, then a woman's voice—indeed old enough to belong to his mother, but not his mother's voice—replied, "Mr. Cordello?"

Even with only two words to go by, Shane detected an accent, vaguely British, in the woman's voice, a clue that helped him not at all in discerning her identity. He didn't know anyone from Great Britain. He only recognized the accent because he was a faithful viewer of *Benny Hill* reruns on cable.

"Yes, this is Shane Cordello," he said, his fear rising to the fore again as his confusion compounded. "Who is this? What's happened?"

There was another pause, then the woman said, "Please hold, Mr. Cordello, for Her Majesty Queen Marissa of Penwyck."

"For who?" he said, certain he must have misunderstood.

"For Her Majesty Queen Marissa of Penwyck," the woman repeated. "Please hold."

Shane balked at the cool command in both the woman's instructions and her voice, and he almost hung up the phone on principle alone. Who did this woman think she was, calling *him*—at work, no less—then telling him to hold? And for the queen of Penwyck? What the hell was that all about? Why hadn't they asked him if he had Prince Albert in a can, too? he wondered, so certain was he that this must be a practical joke.

The only thing that kept him from slamming the receiver back into its cradle was that his curiosity was a more potent force than his pride. Not that he believed for a moment that the queen of Penwyck was about to pick up the phone at the other end of the line, mind you, but clearly this wasn't any run-of-the-mill crank call. No, this was a pretty sophisticated crank call, and Shane wanted to get to the bottom of it. Mainly so he could put an end to it. No sense having the woman call back and rile Mr. Mendoza any further than his employer was already riled. Because the words *employer* and *riled* were two words Shane never wanted to see appearing close together in the same sentence.

After a moment of staccato static and erratic popping—giving him the impression of a genuine long-distance phone call, by golly—a quick click signified that someone had picked up another line. Then a different woman's voice, still old enough to belong to his mother, still not his mother's voice, came over the line.

"Mr. Cordello?" the second woman said. She, too, had an accent, also vaguely British, and a bit more cultivated than the first woman's, if such a thing were possible.

"Yeah, I'm Shane Cordello," he replied with less courtesy than before. "Who the hell are you? And don't bother telling me you're the friggin' queen of Penwyck, lady, 'cause I ain't buyin' it."

There was a stretch of silence from the other end of the line, followed by a single, hasty chuckle. "I have no intention of telling you such a thing, Mr. Cordello."

"Good."

"Because I am not the, ah, friggin'…queen of Penwyck."

"I knew it."

"I am, in fact, the *royal* queen of Penwyck."

Shane rolled his eyes. "Oh, come on, lady, what do you take me for? I wasn't born yesterday, you know."

There was another brief silence, then, "No, I realize that. You were born twenty-three years ago. On April fourteenth. Am I correct?"

Slowly Shane pulled the receiver from his ear and gazed at it with narrowed eyes, as if in doing so, he might force the phone to offer up more information than it was giving him about the woman at the other end of the line. Then, when he realized how ridiculous he must look to his employer, he put the receiver back where it was. "Yeah," he told the woman. "That's my birthday. A matter of public record, too," he added meaningfully. "It still doesn't tell me who you are or what you want."

Instead of a lengthy silence this time, the response from the other end of the line was a weary sigh. "Oh, dear," the woman said, not quite under her breath. "This is going to be a bit more difficult than I thought." Then, "I understand why you might be skeptical, Mr. Cordello," she added. "But I assure you that I am indeed Her Majesty

Queen Marissa of Penwyck. And it is very important that
I speak with you about a very urgent mat—''

"Right," he interrupted again. "If you're the queen of
Penwyck, then I'm the prince of darkness. Tell me another
one."

"Actually, Mr. Cordello, you're not far from the truth,"
the woman said, sounding a bit less imperious than she had
before.

Shane opened his mouth to mutter another disdainful
quip, but what came out instead was "Huh?"

"I said you're not far from the truth," the woman repeated. "Though you're not—quite—the prince of
darkness."

Once again, Shane tried to summons a haughty retort.
And once again, what came out was "Huh?"

"Perhaps it would be better if I let you speak to your
brother, Marcus, first," the woman said.

"Marcus?" Shane echoed, growing even more confused
now.

But instead of hearing the woman's voice in reply again,
Shane was treated to his brother's. "Hello, Shane. It's
Marcus."

The confusion that had been wheeling around in Shane's
head for the last several minutes came to a crashing halt,
crumbling now into a vast heap of bewilderment. "Marcus?" he said, recognizing his brother's voice immediately.
"Where are you? Who was that woman? What the hell is
going on?"

"Answering those questions in order," Marcus said, "as
to the first one, I, uh, I'm in Penwyck. You know Penwyck,
Shane, surely. Small island nation? Near other island
nations of Ireland and Great Britain? It's been in the news
lately because they're forming a military alliance with the
United States. You've heard about that, right?"

"Uh…"

"And I think our mother honeymooned here with husband number three, if memory serves," Marcus continued

blithely. "It's really a beautiful place. Nice people. I mean *really* nice people. Food could be a little spicier. Not that I'm complaining."

Marcus Cordello, Shane knew, was not the kind of man to fool around. His brother hadn't become a millionaire at the age of nineteen by making prank phone calls, and he didn't maintain a multimillion-dollar real-estate empire in one of the nation's largest cities by asking people if they had Prince Albert in a can. No way would Marcus jerk Shane around. If he said he was in Penwyck, then, by God, the man was in Penwyck. And if Marcus was in Penwyck, then that meant that the woman who'd called herself the queen of Penwyck could, by God, very well be—

Uh-oh.

"You're in Penwyck?" Shane echoed miserably.

"I'm in Penwyck," Marcus confirmed.

"The Penwyck that has a Queen Marissa?"

"So you *have* been watching the news," his brother said, clearly holding back a chuckle.

"Um, Marcus?"

"Yes, Shane?"

"Was that really the queen of Penwyck I was talking to on the phone a minute ago?"

"It was indeed."

"The woman I just blew off so royally was really a queen?"

"I'm afraid so."

"So you're standing beside the queen of Penwyck?"

"Yes, I am."

"Is she, um, really, really mad?"

"Define 'really, really,'" Marcus said.

"Like, off-with-his-head mad?"

There was a moment of silence, as if Marcus were contemplating the mood of the woman beside him, a full continent and ocean away from where Shane was standing himself.

"Nah," Marcus said finally.

Shane expelled a soft sigh of relief.

Then, "She'll probably just want to take off your hand when you get here," Marcus added.

"What?" Shane said.

Surprisingly, it wasn't the *take-off-your-hand* part of Marcus's statement that got to Shane most deeply. It was the *when-you-get-here* part that made him take notice.

Then again, Shane thought, why was he surprised by this surprise? Marcus was beginning to make a habit out of dropping bombshells whenever he called. Hell, the last time they'd spoken, his brother had told him there was a possibility that the two of them had been adopted as infants, not that Shane had believed that for a moment. Now Marcus was suddenly in Penwyck, visiting the queen. What next? Would he announce his candidacy for president of the United States? Shane wasn't sure he wanted to know.

"Actually, Her Majesty is a very pleasant woman," Marcus continued, dispelling Shane's troubling thoughts—sort of. "So she might only want a couple of fingers from you, really."

Okay, troubling thoughts were back now.

Shane closed his eyes and lifted a hand to pinch the bridge of his nose, in an effort—a totally futile effort, he soon learned—to ward off a massive headache that seemed to erupt out of nowhere.

"Marcus," he tried again, struggling very hard to maintain his feeble grip on reality. Maybe if he spoke a little more slowly, this conversation would make sense.

And maybe, too, he told himself further, Jennifer Lopez would give him a call this weekend and ask him to go skinny-dipping with her in Puerto Vallarta.

"Marcus," he said once more. "What. Are. You. Talking. About."

Marcus expelled a long, weary sigh from the other end of the line. "What I'm talking about, Shane," he said, "is something you're probably not going to believe. Are you sitting down?"

Shane dropped into his boss's big, comfy chair without even asking permission, and somehow didn't even care when Mr. Mendoza began to glare at him as if this were Shane's last day on earth. Or, at the very least, his last day on the Wellman Towers construction site.

Whatever.

"I'm sitting down," Shane said. "Now tell me what's going on."

"Well," Marcus began, "once upon a time, in a kingdom far away, there lived a beautiful queen and a handsome king who were blessed with a pair of royal twin sons...."

Sara Wallington pushed back the sleeve of her pink cashmere sweater and checked the slim gold watch on her wrist for the sixth time in ten minutes, then sighed heavily with impatience. My, how time crawled when one was having woe, she thought morosely. For there could certainly be nothing *fun* in acting as a glorified nanny for the next twenty-four hours. A nanny for what might potentially be the heir to a throne, granted, but a nanny nonetheless. However, the heir apparently was nowhere to be seen just yet, and they were due to leave L.A. at precisely 11:00 p.m. Right now, it was nearly ten o'clock. Even if they were flying on a private jet, there was a strict departure time they must meet. If the man were any later, they were going to have trouble keeping to their schedule. And she did so loathe not being punctual.

She sighed heavily again, fidgeted with her pearl necklace, twisted the matching pearl stud in one ear and tucked an errant wisp of pale red hair back into her chignon. Then she scanned the hoards of people scampering through LAX like rabid animals and wondered how in the queen's name she was going to find Shane Cordello among them. Of course, it had been Queen Marissa herself who'd gotten Sara into this. A favor, Her Majesty had told Sara's mother in Penwyck when she'd called to see if Sara was available to aid Shane in his travels. Never mind that Sara had finals next month to study for and a term paper to write. She'd escort Mr. Cordello to her native country because her queen commanded it. Favor equaled duty when it came to Her Majesty.

Nevertheless, locating the man was going to be a bit of a task since Sara had been given only a sketchy description of him to go by: brown hair, blue eyes, six-foot-two, one hundred eighty pounds. So she had been able to deduce that he was a largish man, though certainly that wasn't so unique for this vast country of America. Most men here seemed to be big and boisterous and very nearly overwhelming, she had noticed during her four-plus-year stay. Oh, and Shane Cordello was supposed to be rather good-looking, too—according to his brother, at any rate—which ought to make him oh so easy to spot here in Los Angeles where *every*one seemed to be beautiful.

Not much to go on, Sara thought, not for the first time since receiving the queen's phone call this morning. This *morning,* she marveled again, thinking about how much her circumstances had changed in scarcely twelve hours' time. Sara had barely had time to explain the situation to her professors, assuring them she'd return to her classes five days hence, bright and early Monday morning, and would they be so kind as to give her her assignments in advance so that she wouldn't lose too much time.

Now, armed with both her homework and what few belongings she would need for a long weekend in her homeland, Sara waited patiently to meet her destiny. Or, at the very least, to meet Shane Cordello. She was also armed with a handy visual aid, a big white sign, hand-lettered with the word Cordello, to help her in finding that destiny. Or, at the very least, in finding that man. At present, she held the sign waist-high before her, obscuring the simple, camel-colored straight skirt she had coupled with her white blouse and pink cardigan. She boosted the sign a bit higher, at chest height now, hoping that Mr. Cordello wasn't one of those handsome, but not-too-bright males whom one met so frequently in this city.

Not that Sara had spent much time with any men, bright or dim, during her four-and-a-half-year sojourn in this country. College courses did rather limit one's social life, after all, particularly when one was pursuing her master's degree... At least they did if one was serious.

She checked her watch again. Heavens, five minutes had passed this time between glances. She must be vastly enjoying herself now.

"Miss Wallington?"

Sara glanced up at the summons—rather a long way up, too, she couldn't help noticing, which, she supposed, shouldn't surprise her, since she scarcely topped five-foot-two herself—into the face of the man who had just petitioned her. And she immediately realized that *brown hair and blue eyes and rather good-looking* was a description that didn't do the man justice. His hair was, in fact, the color of rich, velvety espresso, and his eyes were an incisive cobalt-blue, reminding her of the darkest depths of the ocean. As for good-looking... Oh, my. That phrase did more than a mere injustice to a man who was, in fact, quite extraordinarily, splendidly, unspeakably, dazzlingly, breathtakingly... She sighed deeply in spite of herself.

Magnificent. That was what Shane Cordello was. In his snug blue jeans and white V-neck T-shirt beneath a faded denim jacket, his low-heeled books scraping over the floor as he shifted his weight from one foot to the other, the man made every system Sara had—and some she hadn't been aware of possessing until this very moment—go on absolute red alert. Never in her life had she encountered a man who made her mouth water. But as she watched his mouth hook into a crooked, wicked little smile, parts of her now—and not just her mouth, either—were feeling very...ah, liquid, indeed.

And when Sara noticed all those changes—in both her body and her very psyche—and when she understood how

Mr. Cordello's mere physical presence in her general vicinity had turned her so readily and thoroughly into a volcano about to burst, the relief she had felt initially upon his arrival suddenly evaporated into... Well, into something else entirely. Something damp and steamy and hot, and altogether inappropriate for a woman who had been asked to perform a favor for her queen. And it simply would not do to experience a cumbersome sort of lust for the man one had been instructed to return to the queen unharassed. Lust, after all, was the one thing that prospective members of the Royal Intelligence Institute did not feel for their charges. It could only—would only—lead to trouble.

"Mr. Cordello," Sara greeted him with as much courtesy—and as little lust—as she could manage. "How delightful to finally make your acquaintance. Queen Marissa has told me much about you."

His expression, which had been rather open and affable before, suddenly changed then, to one of obvious wariness. "She told you about me, huh?" he asked.

Sara nodded. "She said you were quite charming."

Actually, what Her Majesty had said was that Shane Cordello was a man who didn't suffer fools lightly, but one might certainly translate that into charming—if one were frightfully generous about such things, and Sara did pride herself on being a generous person.

"She said that?" Shane Cordello replied dubiously.

"She did indeed," Sara assured him, trying to quell the hot shudder that wound through her whenever he spoke in that rich, rhythmical baritone that very nearly hypnotized her into a narcotic stupor. American accents were so, ah, delightful.

Oh, dear. She really must put a stop to these strange goings-on inside her this instant. "Now, then," she continued in as stalwart a fashion as she could manage. Stalwart, she had always told herself, was a very good thing to be. Even if stalwartness wasn't exactly the most potent boy-magnet in the world, it was still quite the virtue. One should never underestimate the power of a stalwart woman. Ever.

"The jet has been made ready for our takeoff," she said. "Shall we board? Queen Marissa couldn't spare the official royal jet, of course, but she has sent one of the smaller jets. Our sixteen-hour flight to Penwyck will be ever so much more comfortable this way."

Of course, had Her Majesty sent the much larger royal jet, that flight time would have been cut nearly in half, and it would only be approximately ten hours that Sara would be forced to spend with Mr. Very Handsome, Very Interesting Cordello. Providing the larger vessel would have also made it possible for them to arrive in Penwyck at a decent hour, local time. But no. Sixteen hours it would be then, and local arrival time would be approximately... Oh, let her think for a moment... Add eight hours' time difference...plus sixteen...carry the one... Eleven p.m. tomorrow, she finally calculated. Which wouldn't be *too* frightfully indecent an hour, she supposed, if it weren't for the fact that they were both bound to be exhausted from their sixteen-hour flight and wanting desperately to fall into bed.

Fall into *separate* beds, she hastily qualified. *Alone.* Naturally, part of their flight time would be spent on the ground refueling and such, but she and Mr. Cordello would be confined to the very small jet even then. She didn't want to risk losing him now that she had him by allowing him to wander around an airport for any length of time.

Not that she *had* him, Sara quickly corrected herself. Not like...that. Not the way a woman traditionally thought of *having* a man. It wasn't as if the man belonged to her, after all. Nor did she want him, she quickly reminded herself. Or any other man for that matter. But she did so want to keep Mr. Cordello within eyeshot, because if she lost the man who might be king, it would most definitely look bad on any potential résumé she might want to put together. And it went without saying that she *would* have to put together a résumé should she lose Mr. Cordello. Because there was no way the Royal Intelligence Institute would take her on if she bungled an assignment as simple as this.

Sixteen hours, she marveled again, unable to look away from his—oh dear…very interested, she could tell—gaze. Sixteen hours on a nonstop—save brief stops for refueling—course across a continent and an ocean, when each of them clearly found the other…interesting. She was going to be trapped in extremely close confines with this extremely interesting man for sixteen hours.

Of course, they wouldn't be alone during that time, she reminded herself. There would be two pilots and two flight attendants aboard, as well. And the crew's presence would go a long way toward keeping her in line and preventing her from doing anything rash. Something like, oh, say…leaping across the aisle and straddling Mr. Cordello's waist and covering his mouth with her own and kissing him and kissing him and kissing him and…

Where was she? Oh, yes. Sixteen hours. Right. It was a rather long time to be saddling—or rather, saddled *with,* she hastily corrected herself—the man.

Best to think of something else, Sara, she told herself.

She glanced down to see that Mr. Cordello held only one small canvas bag. "Is that all you've brought? Don't you have another bag?"

He, too, glanced down at his burden—unburdensome though it may have been—then back up at Sara. His expression now indicated that he found her question unusual. "Will I need anything more?" he asked. "I didn't get the impression I'd be staying in Penwyck very long. Just long enough to get this ridiculous story straightened out."

During her phone call this morning, the queen had explained to Sara all the particulars of the *ridiculous story,* as Mr. Cordello had referred to it. But Her Majesty wasn't as ready to dismiss the situation as such. Not yet. There was, at present, compelling evidence to suggest that twenty-three years ago, the newborn sons of Queen Marissa and

King Morgan of Penwyck were switched at birth with a pair of different twins.

The way it had been explained to Sara, King Morgan's resentful brother, Broderick, jealous of Morgan because he ascended to the throne when Broderick thought the position should be his, was claiming that he had arranged twenty-three years ago to have the king's rightful heirs kidnapped and placed by adoption with a wealthy family in America immediately after their birth. In their place, he said, he'd had a different set of newborn twins passed off as the king and queen's sons, knowing that neither would be qualified to take control of Penwyck because they weren't descended from royal blood. And that would be the day that Broderick saw his revenge on his brother fulfilled. In the meantime, he'd relished the knowledge that the boys Queen Marissa and King Morgan had raised as their own weren't, in fact, their own sons at all.

Now the queen was beside herself with worry over whether or not Broderick was telling the truth, and whether or not he had been successful in carrying out his plan, and she wouldn't rest until the mystery was solved. The allegedly switched twins had been traced to the Cordello brothers in America, and Her Majesty was adamant that they join her in Penwyck until all was made clear. Marcus Cordello was already in Penwyck, having been accompanied there by Lady Amira Corbin, who had been sent on an errand similar to Sara's. Now it was up to Sara to bring the other Cordello home.

If, in fact, Penwyck was truly his home.

"You don't think you may be one of Her Majesty's missing sons?" Sara asked her Cordello now.

"Hell, no, I don't think so," he retorted. Immediately, however, he looked chastened. "Sorry," he apologized. "Pardon my French."

Sara bit back a smile. "I'm fluent in several languages, Mr. Cordello, one of which happens to be French, and I didn't detect any French in what you just said. However, I accept your apology. Though I assure you, you needn't feel as if you must coddle me. I'm made of firmer stuff than that, I promise you.''

He grinned again at that, but this time it was a grin that told her he didn't believe her for a minute. But that was all right, Sara thought. She knew most men—those who didn't know her well, at any rate—looked at her as if she were a delicate porcelain doll who should be kept constantly under glass. What would Shane Cordello say, she wondered, if he knew the master's degree she was just completing in public administration included minors in tae bahk do and M-16s? Ah, well. No reason to overwhelm the poor man. They'd only be together for—she gulped inwardly—sixteen hours.

"Well, there is apparently substantial evidence, Mr. Cordello, to suggest that the men raised as Prince Dylan and Prince Owen were switched at birth with the rightful heirs to the throne, and that you and your brother, Marcus, may very well be the true princes of Penwyck."

"Horse doodoo," he replied mildly. "To put it bluntly."

Sara laughed. "Thank you so much for sparing my tender sensibilities," she said. And as she said it, her gaze met Shane Cordello's again, holding firm this time, and something in the air between them seemed to crackle and fizz and very nearly explode.

Not good, she thought as a strange heat rippled up her spine and into her chest and down into parts of her that in no way needed warming right now. Not good at all. For sixteen hours, she would be seated beside this man on a very small jet, with no one to bother them save two pilots and two attendants. Pilots and attendants who were trained specifically not to bother the jet's occupants unless those occupants pushed the call button on the arm of their very plush seats.

Sixteen hours, she thought again. Oh, yes. It was going to be a very long flight back to Penwyck indeed.

Two

By the time their jet took off from LAX, it was past one-thirty, so backed up was the air traffic. The moment the wheels left the ground, Shane reminded himself he'd be trapped in this little metal bucket for sixteen hours with only a few infrequent breaks, and told himself to relax. Better yet, he thought, sleep. It had been one helluva day—hell, *two* helluva days—and God knew he was close to exhaustion. But something kept him wide awake—gosh, he couldn't imagine what—so he remained wide-awake, assessing his situation instead.

He replayed everything in his head that Marcus had told him the day before, correlating it with everything the two of them had discussed the last time they spoke. But much of it still made no sense to him. Adopted. That, of course, was what was spinning fastest and foremost in his brain. Marcus and Shane *had* been adopted as newborns, his brother had told him yesterday, because their mother had been unable to conceive. Neither parent had ever seen fit to tell the boys, evidently. The opportunity had never arisen. There had never been any cause. The timing was never right. Take your pick of lame excuses. But Marcus had assured him that their father had verified it when he'd asked for the facts. Still doubtful, however, Shane had tried to call their mother to hear her version of things. But he'd been unable to reach her, and she hadn't returned his call by the time he left his apartment. He'd had to leave a message for her instead.

Adopted. It didn't seem possible, but in hindsight, it explained so many things. Deep down, he believed what his brother had told him. But he hadn't had time to process it all. Adopted. Shane still wasn't sure how he felt about it. On one hand, it changed nothing about his life. On the other hand, it changed everything.

But even that was the least of his worries right now. Because in addition to having been adopted as a newborn, there was a chance—a reasonably good one, evidently—that Shane and Marcus had been born in Penwyck to its rulers, and that they had been switched at birth with a different pair of fraternal twin boys born at roughly the same time. The mother of those boys, then a recently widowed friend of the queen's, had died in childbirth, and the queen had arranged for them to be adopted by a wealthy American couple—Joseph and Francesca Cordello.

Somewhere along the line, though, everything had gone awry. The queen's brother-in-law, Broderick, disgruntled that his brother had inherited the throne instead of him, had instigated a switch of the twins, replacing Owen and Dylan Penwyck with the orphaned boys, and sending the infant princes off to be adopted by the Cordellos in Chicago instead. At least, that was what Broderick was claiming. Queen Marissa, who had known of her brother-in-law's intentions, thought she'd thwarted the plan before it could be carried out, but now, apparently, she had reason to think otherwise. Now, apparently, she had reason to think that maybe the boys she had raised as her own were not her own, and that the American Cordello twins might very well be.

Frankly, the whole situation made Shane's head spin. Even after having had two days to mull it all over, he was still trying to figure out the whys and wherefores and what-the-hells. That was another reason why he had agreed to this trip to Penwyck—just to have explained to him once and for all, hopefully with audiovisual aids, what the hell was going on. He honestly couldn't believe that he and Marcus were the missing heirs to the throne. His gut told him no, and his gut was never wrong. Queen Marissa, too, seemed to think it unlikely, though she did grant there was a possibility. That was why she had insisted on Shane's and Marcus's coming personally to Penwyck, so that they could administer a DNA test on them, in the queen's presence, just to make sure the Cordello twins weren't, in fact, the Penwyck twins. Or vice versa.

Or whatever.

Oh, man, did Shane have a headache now. And he was already exhausted, before his trip had even begun. Sixteen hours, he marveled again. And all of it stuck on a little jet with an escort who seemed disinclined to do anything more than rigorously read big books and sip tea.

The jet might be small, he noted, but it lacked nothing in comfort. He and the prim-and-proper Miss Wallington were the only two passengers on a vessel that was outfitted for a dozen more, and one of the flight attendants had pressed a Scotch and water—damned good Scotch, too, he mused as he enjoyed a second sip—into his hand within moments of him sitting down. Obviously the service was going to be excellent. And the decor was posh and luxurious, reminding him more of a five-star hotel than a jet—not that he had much experience with five-star hotels, not since he was a child at any rate—with oversize seats and plush carpeting down the aisle and pink-tinted lighting to make things easy on the eyes. And his traveling companion…

Well. He certainly had no complaints there, either. Talk about easy on the eyes. When Marcus had called him that morning to go over final preparations for the trip, he'd said the queen was sending an envoy to meet him at LAX who would accompany him to Penwyck. Shane had immediately pictured some doddering old stuffed shirt with a walruslike handlebar mustache decked out in an overly decorated uniform of the Empire. Even when Marcus had said the envoy was named Sara Wallington, Shane had altered his description only slightly, making the stuffed shirt a stuffed blouse, instead. The rest of the description had remained pretty much the same, right down to the mustache, though it hadn't been quite so walruslike on the female version.

But Sara Wallington was in no way walruslike. To put it mildly. No, she was, in fact, one of the most beautiful women Shane had ever laid eyes on. She was also, unfortunately, he was fast realizing, one of the most refined. Dammit. With her crisp, cultivated accent, and her pale red hair twisted up into some kind of bun, and her sea-green eyes currently hidden behind a pair of small, oval-shaped, wire-rimmed reading glasses that she'd donned immediately after sitting down and unfolding the huge tome she currently had open in her lap, she might very well be the owner of this jet, so princesslike was her demeanor.

Still, he didn't think he was the only one who'd felt the little sizzle of heat that had arced between them during their initial encounter. Prim and proper Miss Wallington might be, but there was interest—and more—lying beneath her cool, pink-sweatered facade. And Shane couldn't wait to explore and find out just what that *more* might be.

He stifled a groan. Just what he needed. Trapped in close quarters for sixteen hours with a beautiful woman who was obviously interested in him, too, and she was *exactly* the kind of woman he should avoid. She couldn't be some flashy, fun-loving, devil-may-care hedonist who had as much experience as he had himself and might be amenable to a little short-term fooling around once they arrived in

Penwyck—or even *before* they arrived in Penwyck, he thought further with a lascivious glance at the washroom at the front of the cabin—and then ride off into the sunset with a cheery "Cheerio." No, she had to be some delicate, pearls-wearing, pink-sweater-encased, chaste-looking little nun who would doubtless find it unseemly to break into a sweat. At least, into the kind of sweat that Shane had in mind for the two of them.

She for sure looked like the kind of woman who would want a man to stick around for a while. And not the kind of man Shane was, either. No, Miss Sara Wallington would no doubt want some guy in tweeds and button-downs and riding boots, a man who could say words like *poppycock* and *bumbershoot* with a straight face, a man who would feel more at home viewing pictures in an art gallery while sipping champagne than digging in the dirt on a construction site while anticipating his first Rolling Rock of the evening. A man who would want the same things she probably wanted out of life—commitment, kids, cocker spaniel and the thatched-roof cottage with a cobblestone fence.

Ah, well, Shane told himself philosophically. It wasn't like he didn't have other things to occupy his mind right now, what with all this missing-princes-and-switched-at-birth-and-heir-to-the-throne business going on in his life. Not that it was his mind, necessarily, he'd been thinking of engaging with Miss Pink Sweater over there. Miss Pink Sweater who didn't seem to be any more interested in sleeping than Shane was. Unfortunately, her condition obviously hadn't come about because she was preoccupied by the same lusty thoughts that were trying to preoccupy Shane at the moment. No, it was more because Miss Pink Sweater over there was too busy reading her big book. And daintily sipping her tea. And totally not even noticing he was there.

Dammit.

The problem was, Shane didn't want to occupy his mind with all those other things right now. Maybe not ever. How the hell was a man supposed to react to the news that he might be the heir to a royal throne in a country he'd hardly thought about before? King Shane? Gee, that didn't sound like the appropriate moniker for a blue-collar construction worker whose closest brush with nobility had been his childhood visits to White Castle. There had to have been a royal foul-up somewhere. Still, he hadn't quite been able to turn down Queen Marissa's royal command when she'd insisted he come to Penwyck to join his brother, Marcus, until they could get to the bottom of the mystery.

Hey, if nothing else, Shane thought, he could have a nice little vacation and spend some time with his brother. No matter that he didn't have any vacation time coming. He was pretty sure he'd lost his job anyway, by taking off the way he had yesterday. Mr. Mendoza hadn't looked as if he'd believed the story about King Shane any more than Shane believed it himself.

Inevitably, his gaze stole across the aisle to linger on Sara Wallington again. She really was beautiful, he thought, no matter how tightly she bound herself. The loose sweater and tailored skirt had done nothing to hide her curves, and a few errant wisps of silky hair had fallen from their confinement, giving her the look of a woman who might just be able to let herself go wild once in a while if given the right kind of provocation. Her profile, in the soft light raining down from above her, was elegant and fine, her skin creamy and flawless, touched with just a hint of pink on her high cheekbones. But it was her mouth that caused Shane to feel most restless. Full and delicious looking, all he could do was wonder how she would taste if he touched his lips to hers.

Her head snapped up suddenly then, and she turned to look at him, her gaze falling directly onto his. Her expression was slightly alarmed, as if she'd somehow known what he was thinking about—or maybe she'd been thinking about it, too? he couldn't help wondering—and the pink on her cheeks darkened some when she saw him gazing back at her so resolutely. Instead of calling him on it, however, she only smiled—albeit with a bit of starch.

"Was there something you wanted, Mr. Cordello?" she asked softly.

Oooo, loaded question, Shane thought. What would she do if he answered her truthfully? he wondered. "No, nothing," he lied instead. "I think I have everything I need."

"Excellent," she replied. "Should you think of something…" Her voice trailed off before she finished the remark, as if Shane should know how she'd intended to finish it.

"If I think of something?" he prodded her, a spark of hope flickering to life somewhere inside him. Maybe they *were* on the same wavelength.

She smiled that cool, starchy smile again, and what little spark he'd felt firing suddenly sputtered and died. "Feel free to summon one of the attendants," she finished crisply.

He smiled back, a smile, he felt certain, that was every bit as stiff as hers was. "I'll do that," he assured her. Somehow he refrained from adding *Your Highness,* even though that was exactly the sort of response she seemed to command.

She smiled yet another perfunctory smile, then dropped her gaze back to the book she had opened in her lap. It was a big, thick hardback, probably a textbook, and Shane realized then that she must be a student. Certainly she looked young enough to be, but there was something in her carriage that made her seem like a much older woman, so he hadn't until now realized that she was probably pretty close to his own twenty-three. He told himself not to bother her, because she so clearly wanted to be left alone, but reluctant to consider the prospect of sixteen hours of silence, and still feeling restless for some reason, and still not wanting to think about that possible-prince business, he jump-started their conversation—what little they'd enjoyed so far— again.

"Are you a student?" he asked her.

Very slowly she lifted her head and turned to look at him again. "Of sorts," she said evasively.

"UCLA?" he asked.

She shook her head, but said nothing to enlighten him, as if she didn't want to tell him what school she attended.

"USC?" he tried again.

And again she shook her head. Then, clearly reluctant to divulge even a vague direction to her place of learning, she told him, "I attend a small private college near Santa Barbara."

Woo, now they were gettin' somewhere, Shane thought. That was just *so* specific. "But you're not American, obviously," he said, wanting to know more about her, even if she was evasive and starchy and refined and wearing a pink sweater.

"No, I'm from Penwyck originally," she told him. Adding nothing more to enlighten him.

"You grew up there?"

"Yes," she said. And nothing more.

"So…" he tried again. "What brought you to the States?"

"That small, private college near Santa Barbara," she told him.

"You couldn't major in your specialty in Penwyck?"

When she smiled this time, it was in a way that made Shane think she knew something he didn't know, and that she got great pleasure in the knowing of it. "You could say that," she said. Evasively. Starchily. Refinedly. Pink sweaterishly.

Shane narrowed his eyes at her. Just what was she trying to hide? he wondered. What could she possibly be studying here that she couldn't study in her homeland? Especially since she looked like the kind of woman who would major in English or library science or home ec. Surely they had those things in Penwyck.

"So," he began again.

"Mr. Cordello, I don't wish to be impolite, but I do have

finals next month and quite a bit of work to do before they
arrive. Since I'm obligated to miss my classes for the rest
of this week, I thought the least I might do was take advantage of our flight to get in some study time.''

In other words, Shane translated, *Leave me the hell
alone*.

He lifted both hands, palm out, in a gesture of surrender.
''Sorry,'' he said, finding it hard to feel apologetic. ''Don't
want to distract you from your studies. I'll just, um—'' he
glanced at the call button on the arm of his seat ''—summon the attendant. How will that be?''

And before Miss Pink Sweater, Finals-to-Study-For Wallington could say another word, one of the flight attendants
appeared at Shane's side, obviously ready at his beck and
call. And although she was by no means a princess—unlike
some people, he thought morosely—the attendant was
quite...fetching. Fetching in the dark, curvy way he liked
for women to be fetching, too, and *not* wearing a pink
sweater and pearls. Fetching enough that she might very
well make the next sixteen hours more bearable. If Shane
played his cards right.

Sara read over page 548 of *Detente and Diplomacy for
a New Millennium* for perhaps the sixteenth time and tried
not to notice how tantalizing was the sound of Shane Cordello's rough, rich laughter. It was much more appealing
than the flight attendant's laughter—which Sara found
much too high-pitched and much too obvious—that was
certain. And Sara should know. She'd been listening to both
of them laugh for the better part of fourteen hours now.

Of course, there had been a few breaks in the hilarity
during that length of time, periods when Sara and Mr. Cordello had slept with dubious success, and periods when the
jet had landed to refuel and restock, and periods when the
cabin crew had taken breaks. But for the most part, Shane
Cordello and Fawn the flight attendant—honestly, Sara
thought, as if *any*one on board actually believed that was

her *real* name—had gotten on swimmingly. And if there had been moments when Sara had found herself grinding her teeth and swallowing her irritation, well… It was only because Fawn had one of those tittering laughs that could drive any sane person to drink.

Of course, Sara realized she had only herself to blame. She had, after all, fairly chased Mr. Cordello into Fawn's clutches by treating him so shabbily since meeting him. But she hadn't been able to help herself. He confused her, made her feel things she wasn't used to feeling, things she didn't *want* to feel. In doing so, he'd raised her defenses, as well. And when Sara's defenses were raised, she wasn't the most accommodating person in the world. No, actually, she was the most fearful. And her fear always made her behave badly.

Oh, when *would* they be landing? she wondered, checking her watch. It was now nearing 3:00 p.m. Thursday, West Coast time, so they must be within two hours of Penwyck. Absently, she adjusted the time on her watch to reflect the Meridian Time Zone, which would now put them at 10:45 p.m. Penwyck time.

She'd probably do well to try and sneak in another nap before they landed, she thought, since she would no doubt have little opportunity to really sleep until dawn. Once the jet landed—in the dead of night, she couldn't help reminding herself morosely—she and Mr. Cordello would be met by members of the Royal Intelligence Institute. But she was under royal edict to stay with Mr. Cordello herself until she could hand-deliver him to Queen Marissa and his brother. Those two would almost certainly be in bed asleep by the time they arrived, which meant that Sara would be obligated to keep an eye on Mr. Cordello until morning. They could eat a proper meal at the palace, she thought, then exchange pleasantries until Her Majesty joined them. Or, if Mr. Cordello wanted to sleep himself, Sara could… She sighed heavily. She supposed she could stand in the doorway of his room and watch him sleep. Because she had promised Queen Marissa she would not leave the man's side until he was safely delivered to Her Majesty.

Sara reached for her cup of Earl Grey, then decided that she'd consumed enough tea on this flight to float the entire India Company, and that a glass of champagne would be most welcome now. She pushed the buzzer to summon the attendant—oh, what rotten luck, it was Fawn on duty, and now the poor thing would be forced to end her conversation…and effusive tittering…with Shane Cordello—in an effort to order a drink. And although poor Fawn did her best to hide her irritation at being so put-upon as to perform her job, it seemed to take an inordinate amount of time for Sara to finally get her drink.

Honestly. Good help was so hard to find these days.

As Fawn—the darling girl—retreated to the minibar, Shane Cordello returned to his seat opposite Sara's. He was wearing a smile that was much too smug for her liking, but he didn't seem too much the worse for wear. He did look tired, though, Sara noted, his hair rumpled—adorably so, she couldn't help thinking—and faint purple crescents smudging his eyes. She doubted she looked much better, having worn the same clothes for more than twenty-four hours now, but somehow, he didn't make her feel as if she should be discomfited by the fact. His own white T-shirt and jeans were as rumpled as his hair, but on him, somehow, the look worked to his advantage.

All in all, Sara thought, with his untidy clothes and his tousled hair and his heavy-lidded eyes, and his day's growth of dark beard, he looked like a man who wanted to collapse into bed…with a willing woman…and get absolutely no sleep while he was there.

A strange, languorous heat wound through her as she envisioned him doing exactly that, with—oh, dear—herself cast in the role of the willing woman. Immediately, Sara banished the graphic image from her brain. But remnants of it lingered, scorching the edges of her mind, and no matter how hard she tried, she couldn't banish it completely.

"So, Miss Wallington," Mr. Cordello began in that luscious voice, smiling his delicious smile, "how much longer 'til we get there?"

Sara lifted her champagne to her mouth for a quick—but substantial—sip. "Not too, I should think," she told him when she completed the action, the velvety liquid warming her throat, her chest, her belly and points beyond. Oh, no, wait, she thought. It wasn't the champagne warming those points beyond. No, it was Shane Cordello's smile that was doing that. Oh, dear. "No, ah…no more than an hour or two I would imagine," she managed to add in a voice that she was relieved to realize didn't make her sound *too* awfully feeble-minded.

His smile seemed to grow even more dangerous somehow, and Sara couldn't help thinking that he had almost certainly picked up on that *points beyond* business. Probably because of her not *too* awfully feeble-minded voice.

His verbal response, however, wasn't quite in keeping with that dangerous smile. "Wanna play Twenty Questions?" he asked.

Sara arched her brows curiously. "I beg your pardon?"

Mr. Cordello lifted his shoulders and let them drop in a shrug that she supposed he meant to look casual, but somehow it didn't. "Twenty Questions," he repeated. "It's a game my brother and I used to play as kids to pass the time on long car trips." His expression went a bit grim when he added, "Or to drown out the noise of our parents' shouting at each other there at the end."

Tactfully, Sara pretended she hadn't heard that last part, and focused on the first part instead. "You and your brother must be very close. Being twins and all, I mean."

"Actually, our closeness has less to do with being twins than it does being cast adrift at an early age."

"I'm not sure I follow you," Sara said.

"Our folks split up when Marcus and I were nine. Marcus went to live with our father, and I went to live with our mother.''

A pang of something sharp and unpleasant twisted Sara's midsection, and she was surprised to realize how very much she cared about what had happened to this man she had only just met. ''That must have been very difficult for you both,'' she said softly.

He expelled an exasperated sound. ''To put it mildly. We were able to spend a month together every summer, but it never felt like enough. Even now, I wish we had more time to spend together.''

''Yet, as adults, you live hundreds of miles away from each other,'' Sara couldn't help pointing out.

Mr. Cordello shrugged again, almost apologetically this time. ''My mother has made Southern California her home, and I don't want to be too far away from her. She's—'' He halted abruptly.

''What?'' Sara asked before she could stop herself, knowing it was impolite to pry. Even if Mr. Cordello *had* been the one to bring it up.

He expelled a weary breath. ''She's… She's not very… She has a habit of…'' Now he uttered a restless sound. ''Let me put it this way. She's on husband number five, and none of them since my father have been much of a prize. Even my father didn't do right by her, as far as I'm concerned. But at least he loved her. For a while. She's just not good at taking care of herself,'' he finally concluded. ''She needs someone close by to keep an eye on her. On things,'' he quickly corrected himself. ''So as long as she calls L.A. home, that's where I'll be, too.''

Something inside Sara turned over a little bit at hearing his admission. He was a good son. He wanted to make certain his mother was well cared for. In spite of his rough outward appearance, he had a protective, gentle streak inside. She never would have guessed that. And knowing it now…

Well. Knowing it now only made him that much more

dangerous, Sara thought. Because it made him that much more appealing. That much more interesting. That much more likable. And she couldn't afford to like Shane Cordello. She just couldn't. Circumstances being what they were, it couldn't possibly go anywhere. She had a career all mapped out, one she hadn't even had the opportunity to embark upon yet, and it did *not* include the addition of another human being in her life. And Mr. Cordello might very well be embarking on a new career of his own—heir to a kingdom—one that would turn his entire life upside down. The best either of them could hope for would be something temporary at best. And what would be the point in that?

"Twenty Questions," Sara said, backpedaling. "How is it that you play such a game?"

Mr. Cordello seemed not to understand the question at first, because he was clearly still lost in memories of his brother and his mother and the mix of everything those two created inside him. Then suddenly he smiled, a smile that was at once relieved and regretful. "I think of something, and you can ask me twenty questions that I have to answer 'yes' or 'no' to. If you can't guess what I'm thinking about with twenty questions, I win. If you *do* guess before you reach twenty, you win. Or we could do it the other way around. You think of something, and I get to ask you questions until I guess what it is you're thinking."

Sara gazed at him again, more studiously this time, considering his blue eyes, his full, succulent mouth, the overly long dark hair that was just begging for a woman's fingers to sift through it. Lowering her gaze surreptitiously, she noted the way the sleeves of his T-shirt strained over salient biceps, and the rich, dark hair that sprung from the V-neck. Then higher again, over the strong column of his throat and the sculpted jaw, darkened and coarsened now by his uncivil beard. And for some reason, she found herself wondering how it would feel to have her own delicate skin abraded by his.

"Maybe you should start," she said. "You think of something first, and I'll ask you questions."

Because God knew there was no way that Sara wanted him delving into her own thoughts just now.

Three

Oh, man. Shane was ninety-nine percent sure he could tell what Miss Sara Wallington was thinking right now, without having to ask her a single question. Because, whether she realized it or not, she was giving off clues like nobody's business. Really good clues, too. Clues he wanted very badly to pick and run with. Maybe that washroom at the front of the cabin could prove useful after all…

The thought was just forming in his brain when the small jet suddenly gave a lurch. Automatically, Shane gripped the arms of his seat, but not before he was thrown sideways by another jolt. Then forward by another. And backward by another. Immediately, his gaze flew to Sara's. ''What the hell was that?'' he asked.

She shook her head, her expression—and her ferocious stranglehold on the arms of her own seat—indicating that she was clearly as alarmed as he. But where Shane would have expected someone in a pink sweater and pearls and a bun to fasten her seat belt and start wringing her hands and muttering something like, "We're all going to die, we're all going to die," what Sara Wallington did was leap up from her seat and march forward, stating in no uncertain terms, "I have no idea what the hell that was, but I intend to find out."

No sooner had she stood, however, than the jet began to execute a fierce turn, something that threw her right back into her seat in an awkward sprawl. For one long moment, the jet banked so sharply and so swiftly that neither of them could rise from their seats. When the vessel finally did come out of the turn, though, Sara immediately jumped up again and began her forward march once more.

Shane was about to leap up right behind her when Fawn the flight attendant came striding down the aisle toward them, brushing one hand over the backs of the seats as she came, as if she were preparing for another one of the jet's odd maneuvers. Reluctantly, he eased back into his seat, because he figured she was going to reassure them that everything was fine, they'd just hit a little turbulence, had had to change course to avoid more, and how about another Scotch or champagne to tide them over for the remainder of the flight, hmm? But instead of reassuring them, as the curvy brunette drew nearer, she whipped out a small automatic pistol and pointed it right at Sara's heart.

All in all, it wasn't a development that Shane had anticipated.

"You'll do well to take your seat, Miss Wallington," Fawn said in an even cooler, crisper tone than Sara had been using herself on this flight. And that was saying something. "Otherwise," she added just as coldly, "I shall be obliged to shoot you."

And again Shane's pink-sweater-and-pearls-wearing companion surprised him. "Oh, I don't *think* so," she said coolly as she stepped forward, and in one fluid effort disarmed the other woman with a good swift kick to her hand. Without hesitation, Sara then scooped up the dropped weapon, grabbed the flight attendant and spun her around into a chokehold that would have done Hulk Hogan proud, and pointed the weapon right at Fawn's head.

Shane's mouth dropped open in astonishment, but before he could say a word, the other flight attendant—a man—and one of the pilots, likewise a man, appeared in the aisle beyond Sara and Fawn, each of them armed with their own weapons.

"Release her and sit down, Miss Wallington," one of the men said.

As he spoke, Fawn began to struggle with Sara, and in the ensuing altercation, Sara dropped the pistol again, but tore the sleeve of the flight attendant's uniform. On her exposed forearm, Fawn bore a tattoo, an ugly black dagger, which was something Shane thought an odd choice for a woman like her. He would have had her pegged for a long-stemmed rose. Or a unicorn, maybe. Something fluffy and harmless.

Until Sara, too, noted the mark and said, "I should have known. Black Knights."

Her voice dripped with contempt when she said it, leading Shane to believe she knew exactly what she was talking about, even if he was totally clueless.

"Of course we're Black Knights," the male flight attendant agreed with an evil smile, holding his gun steady on Sara as Fawn scooped up the dropped weapon and did likewise with it. "Who else would we be?"

"Dissidents," Sara said, and Shane knew she was providing the information for his benefit. "They're traitors to the crown."

Fawn made a soft tsking sound in objection. "Please, Miss Wallington," she said. "We're activists, not traitors."

"Oh, yes, I forgot," Sara agreed bitterly. "You actively participate in dissension, treason and terrorism. Sorry for the confusion."

"We have a very noble cause," Fawn told her. "We want independence for the people of Penwyck."

"The people of Penwyck are already independent," Sara said.

"They won't be if this alliance with Majorco goes through," the pilot objected. "And joining with the United States for any reason is certain to make the country dependent on the evil empire."

"Oh, please." It wasn't Sara who took exception this time, but Shane. "Evil empire?" he added. "C'mon, guys. Drag yourselves into the twenty-first century already."

But the Black Knights ignored him—except for the pilot, who aimed his pistol directly at Shane's head.

"Fascists," Sara spat at them. "You'll never win, you know. Your only support comes from within. The people of Penwyck love their king and queen and trust them to do what's best for the country, as indeed they will. You're nothing but scum, all of you."

At that, Fawn stepped forward, doubled her fist and backhanded Sara as hard as she could across the face. "We will succeed in our cause," she said levelly as Sara immediately straightened again.

And Shane had to hand it to the pink sweater, because Sara didn't so much as raise a hand to her face to acknowledge the strike. He, on the other hand, lurched out of his seat with the intention of charging Fawn, stopping only when the pilot extended his arm meaningfully, sharpening his aim. Shane honestly wasn't sure what he'd planned to do when he'd reacted as he had. He'd certainly never considered himself to be the kind of man capable of striking a woman. But he also knew there was no way in hell he'd let anyone get away with hitting Sara Wallington.

Not unless, you know, they pulled a gun on him.

Sara extended an arm across the aisle to stop Shane from going too far, even before he stopped himself. "It's all right," she told him.

"The hell it is," he retorted, still poised for attack, his entire body humming with the adrenaline that pumped through it. He couldn't begin to understand what was going on, but the danger was clear, and he was naturally itching to do something about it. The problem was he just couldn't imagine *what* to do that wouldn't end up with a gunshot wound to either him or Sara, or both, one that might potentially be fatal.

"It's pointless to fight them," Sara said, clearly speaking to Shane. "They outnumber us, and they'll kill us both without a thought."

"Indeed we will," Fawn said, angling her gun on Sara again.

Which, Shane had to admit, was infinitely more effective in keeping him at bay than pointing a gun at him was, something Fawn obviously realized. Dammit.

"In fact," she added, "I don't see why we need to keep you alive anyway. We have the diamonds we came after, after all."

"Fawn!" the pilot rasped. "You stupid git! Don't say another word!"

The flight attendant looked properly chastened, but a bitter fire still burned in her eyes.

"Diamonds?" Sara asked. "I've never known the Black Knights to take an interest in fine jewelry."

Evidently unable to keep herself quiet, Fawn piped up again, "They're to finance—"

"Fawn!" the pilot interjected once more. "Shut your trap."

"Yes, do, please, Fawn," Sara cajoled. "You're becoming tedious."

Fawn doubled her fist and raised her hand once more, and Shane prepared to spring forward to... Do something in retaliation. But the other flight attendant tugged Fawn backward, nudging her behind himself, and took her place instead.

"Sit," the pilot told Sara as if he were speaking to a cowering spaniel. "Sit, Miss Wallington, or die. And if you die, then where will that leave the future king of Penwyck, eh?"

"I'm not the future king," Shane quickly pointed out. "I'm just a construction worker from SoCal who'd rather be surfing."

The man turned his attention to Shane and grinned an evil little smile. "Well, we don't know that for sure, now, do we? And neither do the king and queen. Oh, you have value to us, Mr. Cordello. You have no idea how much. Now return to your seats," the man repeated. "We'll be landing shortly."

"Where?" Sara demanded.

He chuckled. "As if we'd tell you." Then he smiled. "All right. Not Penwyck. There. That should narrow it down for you."

"And what will happen when we get there?" Sara commanded.

The man's smile broadened. "You ask too many questions, Miss Wallington. You and Mr. Cordello are safe for the time being, provided you do exactly as you are told and don't try to escape. But if you try anything improper, we will kill you." He turned his icy gaze on Shane then, too. "Both of you. In the world of the Black Knights, all people are created equal, whether they be a mere student or heir to the throne."

"Meaning all life is equally cheap to you," Sara said flatly.

In reply, the man only turned his gaze back to her and smiled that grim smile again.

And somehow Shane knew that none of it was true. Not that the Black Knights were activists. Not that all people were created equal in their world. Not that their cause was a noble one. Not that he and Sara were safe.

And not that Sara was a mere student, either. He just wished he knew for sure who—and what—she really was.

Sara wasn't surprised when she exited the jet approximately two hours later—with her hands bound behind her back and her cheek throbbing from where the ferocious

Fawn had struck her—to find that they had landed on a deserted, poorly lit tarmac out in the middle of nowhere. Of course, she couldn't be positive that two hours had passed, but she was reasonably sure that was how long they had remained in flight after the hijacking. She'd been forced to guesstimate the passage of time, as the Black Knights had taken her watch. And her pearls. And her textbooks. And her purse and luggage. And her shoes.

Strangely, it was the textbooks about which she was most concerned. She did hope the Black Knights didn't examine them too closely. And she hoped she got them back eventually. They'd been frightfully expensive.

She had only been able to guess at what their final destination might be, as well, though she had done her best to gauge the jet's direction at one point by opening the screen over the window beside her seat and noting the position of the moon and stars. Unfortunately, one of the terrorists had seen what she was doing—hence her tied hands—and had slammed the screen back down again. Before he'd managed to do so, however, Sara had been able to discern with some confidence that they had been heading southeast. Which would have put them in Spain, or perhaps Portugal.

Nevertheless, with it being night, she had been unable to determine anything in the landscape that might have proven to be a landmark—no mountains, no shorelines, no lakes, nothing. The air was cooler and crisper than what she was accustomed to, not to mention surprisingly windy, leading her to believe they were at a higher elevation than one might find in Penwyck. But with so many variables in place, she honestly couldn't say with any real certainty where they were.

Of one thing, however, she was completely certain: she and Shane could be dead by dawn if they didn't behave exactly as they were told.

The Black Knights were a nasty group, completely without morals or scruples. They *wouldn't* balk at killing a young student or a man who might be king. They wouldn't balk at killing anyone. Over the last decade, they'd been responsible for a number of assassination attempts on King Morgan, and numerous episodes of political sabotage. Oh, they'd started off as a small faction of seemingly ineffective upstarts, but it hadn't been long before they'd organized into a formidable enemy of the crown. They were even suspected of kidnapping Prince Owen of Penwyck, and Sara couldn't help wondering now just how deeply their involvement had run in a number of other intrigues that had plagued the royal family over the years. Certainly they were capable of just about anything.

Her right cheek throbbed again, reminding her that she probably had a very impressive black eye by now. Honestly, she wouldn't have thought the tittering Fawn would have even known how to make a fist, let alone use one. Just the first of many mistakes that Sara now realized she had been making since leaving L.A. The first had been in trusting that the crew who boarded Her Majesty's jet in L.A. were the same ones who regularly flew with the royal family—clearly, they were not. The second had been in assuming that their flight would be a boring, uneventful one—clearly, it had not been.

Sara mentally berated herself yet again. Good heavens, the most important lesson she'd learned as a first-year student had been "Trust no one and nothing." But no. She had been under the spell of Shane Cordello, too wrapped up in dreamy fantasies about his blue eyes and silky hair and what it would be like to—

Drat it all, she was doing it again. It was no wonder they were in their current predicament, so foolishly and school-girlishly had she been behaving. Well, no more of that. Sara Wallington would not be caught with her pants down again. To put it in the charming American slang.

The Black Knights had by now herded Shane off the jet, and she saw that, although they'd allowed him to don his denim jacket, they'd taken his shoes, too. And, like Sara, his hands were bound behind his back, as well. They'd separated the two of them after that initial confrontation, putting Shane at the front of the cabin and Sara in the back. He didn't seem much the worse for wear at the moment, she noted, though he did look even more tired—and angry—than he had before. When he glanced over at her, his expression went harder still, and she realized his focus lingered on her cheek. Oh, yes. Even in the darkness, she must look like the very devil—or, at the very least, like the new world heavyweight champion—if his expression was any indication.

The biggest of the Black Knights pushed him toward Sara, and Shane stumbled a bit before regaining his equilibrium and righting himself once more. Somehow he seemed even larger as he completed the action, as if he were flexing every one of his—not unimpressive—muscles as he straightened. His expression was murderous when he stood upright again, and it occurred to Sara that, between the two of them, if no others joined the dissidents, they might stand a chance of escape. All she had to do was plan well. And wait for the proper moment. And hope that Shane Cordello was as good as he looked.

Ah, for escape plans, she meant.

"You okay?" he asked softly when the Black Knight who had shoved him toward Sara returned to his compatriots and began to confer with them in low tones.

She nodded, thinking his concern was sweet...before halting herself from thinking about him at all. No need to get lost down that route again. She'd already caused enough trouble that way. "I'm fine," she told him quietly. "Just feeling very stupid at the moment."

He looked puzzled. "Why should you feel stupid?"

"Because I should have been prepared for something like this," she told him. "I never should have allowed it to happen."

His expression grew even more confused. "How could you possibly have been prepared for something like this?

And why should the responsibility for it happening be yours anyway?''

In response, Sara only shook her head. Things were much too complicated to try and explain it all to him at present.

"What's going to happen to us now?" he asked. But he didn't sound fearful or anxious when he voiced the question. No, there was only hostility and contempt in his tone.

"I imagine they'll hold us hostage while they make their demands," she told him.

"What kind of demands?"

"Judging by their comments on the jet, they'll threaten to harm you if Penwyck doesn't cancel its alliances with Majorco and America."

"You mean it's my fault that we're in this situation."

She looked at him, surprised. "I didn't say that."

"You didn't have to."

"Shane, I'm not blaming you for this."

"I know. You're blaming yourself."

"I'm blaming those bastards who hijacked the plane and took us hostage. No one else."

"But if I hadn't come…"

He left the sentence unfinished. Not that it needed finishing. In spite of that, Sara wanted to finish it for him, wanted to point out that if he hadn't come, then she never would have met him, never would have seen his beautiful blue eyes or his bewitching smile that made her heart turn over, or—

Drat. She truly must put an end to all this fantasizing, or else the two of them really would be dead by dawn.

"Neither of us could have known something like this would happen," she said.

He inhaled a deep breath, as if he were going to argue with her again. Instead, though, he only asked, "So what happens after they make their demands?"

Sara tried to smile reassuringly, but she had a feeling the gesture fell well short of its mark. "I wish I could tell you that we'll be safe until those demands are met or refused, but I can't be certain about our safety at all. Nothing is certain with this group. They're a ghastly bunch. And I *can* tell you that their demands, regardless of what they are, will almost certainly be refused, because the royal family has a zero tolerance when it comes to dealing with the Black Knights.'' She hardened her expression, so that he would understand she was perfectly serious when she told him, ''They're capable of anything. Even murder.''

''You talk like you know a lot about them,'' Shane said.

Oh, she knew more than he realized, Sara thought. She'd made it her life's work to know about the Black Knights and other factions like them. She intended to make a career out of disbanding and punishing such groups. That small, private college near Santa Barbara that she attended was a world-renowned facility for counterterrorist training. But, of course, there was no reason why Shane needed to know that. In fact, the less he knew about her, the better off they'd both be.

''I'm from Penwyck,'' she said by way of an explanation. ''Everyone in Penwyck knows about the Black Knights. They've gone out of their way over the years to make their presence there known.'' Which was certainly true, Sara reminded herself. So she wasn't voicing a deception to Shane when she said it. Not really.

He had opened his mouth to say something more, but he closed it again suddenly, staring at something in the distance behind Sara. When she turned to follow his gaze, she saw two automobile headlights bearing down on them from a few hundred feet down the tarmac. They ended up being attached to a big, black Mercedes sedan that seemed not to emerge from the dark night so much as it did become a part of it. The windows, too, were darkened by tinting, so she couldn't see who was driving. One of the Black Knights approached the car as it rolled to a stop, but the window went down just a few centimeters—enough to allow conversation between driver and terrorist that was too quiet for Sara to hear.

After a few moments—and what appeared to be a rather heated exchange, she couldn't help noticing—the Black Knight turned to his companions and signaled them to escort Sara and Shane into the back seat of the car. Of course, they didn't so much escort the two of them as they did manhandle and dump them, but the end result was the same. Sara and Shane were forced into the back of the car between two of the Black Knights, behind a smoked glass screen that prohibited them from seeing the occupants of the front seat, a point which soon became moot anyway, as she and Shane were promptly blindfolded.

The group rode in silence for a good half hour, Sara deduced, all of it uphill, she also noticed, until the car finally came to a stop. Still blindfolded, she and Shane were shepherded out of the car and across what felt like a grassy yard, to an unevenly cobbled walkway. Then she was nudged up three steps—wooden steps, because they creaked and felt warped—and through a door that was then closed, and ominously locked, behind her. She felt Shane's presence through all of this, even though no one spoke a word. She thought the Black Knights would separate the two of them, but they were both shoved into a room together. Then she heard another door closed, and locked, behind them, followed by the sound of receding footsteps and muffled voices. And then she realized that she and Shane were alone for the first time in hours. Well, alone in a room, at any rate. She was certain they were still under guard stationed elsewhere in the building.

The room where they found themselves smelled dusty and faintly of cinnamon, and Sara sensed that the dimensions were quite small. Her suspicion was confirmed when, in just two small steps, she bumped into what seemed to be shelves. Empty shelves. Four steps in the opposite direction had her bumping into more.

"Shane," she said softly. Only after voicing the word

aloud did she realize it was the first time she had called him by his given name, and she couldn't help grinning a little wryly. She supposed there was nothing like being taken hostage with someone to breed immediate intimacy with him.

"What?" he whispered back.

"Are you all right?"

"Gee, except for being tied up, blindfolded and taken hostage by dissident traitors, not to mention exhausted, thirsty and starving to death, yeah. I'm just peachy keen."

Well, at least he hadn't lost his sense of humor, Sara thought. Sort of. "I'm going to move toward you," she said. "When I'm standing in front of you, use your teeth to remove my blindfold. Then I'll turn around and you must untie my hands."

He said nothing in response to that, something Sara found curious. She would have thought he'd want to be free of his bonds, and he couldn't be free of them until she was free of hers. Perhaps he'd received a blow to the head at some point in the evening, she thought, and now his wits were addled.

"Shane?" she said again.

"What?" he grumbled.

"Can you do as I've asked?"

He hesitated a moment, then snapped, "You haven't *asked* me to do anything. You're issuing orders like a drill sergeant."

Strangely, she felt a giggle bubble up at that. Oh, dear. All the exhaustion and tension and upheaval of the last two days were definitely catching up with her. She was getting hysterical. *Now, now, Sara, none of that,* she cautioned herself. Still, she couldn't quite keep the—albeit erratic—laughter from her voice when she replied, "Well, my goodness, aren't we just behaving like the slighted debutante?"

"Debutante, hell," Shane retorted. "I just don't see who died and made you general."

"Well, the family name *is* Wallington," she reminded him. "It's not such a far cry from Wellington."

There was another curious silence from him, then, "Oh. Well. Yeah. Okay. But I still don't see why you're suddenly the one in charge."

Sara bit back an exasperated sound. Men. Honestly. They were such delicate creatures. Trying again, she said—in a sweeter tone this time—"Please, Mr. Cordello, if you could be so kind, I'd very much appreciate your liberating me from my bonds. If it pleases you, I'll move in your general direction, and if you have a moment to spare, perhaps you could orally remove my blindfold, hmm? Would that be doable, do you think? It makes more sense, after all, since you're the taller of us. I might have a bit of a problem using my mouth on you."

And oh, how she wished she hadn't said those last words, Sara thought immediately after voicing them. Because even though she had *not* meant them the way they sounded, and even in their current situation, when she should have her mind on a million other things, the thought of using her mouth on Shane was just too, too tempting not to consider it. As if she even had a choice in the matter. Because try as she might since meeting him, Sara had been unable to think of little other than Shane Cordello. Now, bringing her mouth into it…

Oh, dear.

He seemed to be thinking about her using her mouth on him, too, because yet another silence ensued, and it was infinitely more awkward than any of the others had been. She was actually grateful to hear him eject another impatient sound when he finally did, because it told her that he, at least, was able to move his mind on to other matters. At least she hoped that was what it meant. She'd hate to think that he was thinking about her using her mouth on him as she was thinking about using her mouth on him and feeling impatient as a result. Unless of course, that impatience resulted from the fact that he was so anxious for the two of them to get down to—

Drat. She was doing it *again*. Thinking errant, erotic thoughts about Shane Cordello. While being held hostage, no less. What on earth was *wrong* with her?

"You don't have to pour it on so thick, Miss Wallington," he finally said, and with the mention of pouring thickness, her thoughts once again turned to the, ah, unacceptable. Then she realized he was talking about flattery and not— Ah…he was talking about something other than what she was thinking about. "I'm not a child," he added petulantly.

Oh, she was frightfully aware of that. But all she offered in response to his assurance was a noncommittal "Mmm."

"Come over here," he said.

And there was something in his voice, something velvety and seductive and rough, that sliced through the darkness and made her skin fairly prickle with anticipation. What an odd reaction, Sara thought. Odder still was the way she so automatically and immediately moved toward him. Because she realized she was responding to his command *not* because it was one she had initially proposed herself, but because this time he was the one uttering it. And somehow, with that one simple utterance, everything between them changed.

Sara moved forward uncertainly, sensing where he was without seeing him. And blindfolded as she was, she realized she was acutely aware of him in ways she hadn't been initially. She could smell him now, a musky mix of manly scents that combined to put her senses on red alert. And she registered his breathing, deep and low and a little ragged. As she drew nearer still, she felt the heat of his body mingling with her own, and the very air surrounding them seemed to grow damp and heavy with it. And she quickly recognized the fact that she'd misjudged his distance when she bumped softly into him, her front to his.

Somehow, though, she couldn't quite make herself take

even a tiny step backward. She told herself it was because she needed to be this close to him in order for him to perform the action she had requested—oh, all right, commanded—that he perform. Then she had to force herself to admit that although she did indeed *need* to be this close to him, that need hadn't necessarily come about because she wanted him to free her bonds. No, her need in that moment stemmed from something else entirely, something Sara told herself she'd be better off not pondering.

He was taller than she remembered, perhaps because she no longer wore the low heels she had initially been wearing, and his chin grazed the crown of her head when they made their first contact. It occurred to her then that this was the first time the two of them had actually physically touched each other, and somehow that made the gesture seem almost poignant.

Before Sara had a chance to consider anything else, she felt his lips brushing over her forehead, and she realized he was doing just as she had asked—or, rather, commanded—he do, trying to remove her blindfold with his mouth. But he had trouble finding it at first. His coarse, unshaven jaw grazed her forehead and temple, and she remembered then how she had wondered what such a touch would feel like. Now, suddenly, she knew. It felt exquisite. Seductive. Arousing. His mouth began brushing against her sensitive flesh then, again over her forehead and temple, a good half-dozen times before he finally gripped the scrap of cloth with his teeth. And with every soft brush of his lips against her skin, with every faint breath that warmed her flesh, her heart gathered speed and beat more frantically against her ribs.

Good heavens, she thought. How could he possibly be making her feel aroused at a time like this? Before she had time to consider that question, he had tugged her blindfold down from her eyes, then lower still, over her nose and mouth, until he could bend over enough that the fabric hung loosely around her neck. She couldn't be sure in the dark, but he seemed not to straighten right away, but lingered a bit, inhaling deeply. She felt his warm breath dampen her sensitive flesh, and if she hadn't known better, she would have sworn he dragged his open mouth lightly along the slender column of her throat before he rose to his full height again. Surely, though, that had only been a product of her overly heated imagination. Hadn't it?

Oh, good God, what had come over her?

"You smell good," he said as he pulled slowly away from her, surprising her. "You smell…sweet."

And although the exchange seemed completely inane considering their circumstances, Sara felt helpless not to respond. "It's, ah… I suppose it's the, um, the toiletries I use. They're…um…" She expelled a nervous chuckle before finally managing to conclude, "It's lavender."

In the darkness, she could discern nothing of Shane's expression, but somehow she thought he smiled. "It's nice," he whispered. And something in that whisper warmed her entire body, inside and out.

She swallowed with some difficulty, then turned her back to him. "Can you, ah—" She halted abruptly when she realized how rough her voice sounded, then took a deep breath and tried again. "Can you reach the ropes round my wrists?" she asked.

She felt him turn around, too, and lifted her hands as much as she could, to the small of her back. He stooped down some, to meet her halfway, and she felt his fingers fumbling over the heavy nylon line they had used to bind them both. It took some doing, and a good amount of time passed as he worked at the loops and knots, but finally Sara felt the bonds loosening. She, too, began to work her hands and fingers, and with one final tug from Shane, and a last jerk of her own hand, she managed to free herself.

Hastily, she shook the ropes to the floor, untied the blindfold from around her neck and tossed it aside, then went to work on the cords wrapped around Shane's wrists. She had him freed in no time, and he immediately reached up to loosen his own blindfold. Even without the benefit of light, she knew he ripped it from his face and hurled to the floor as if it were the most despicable thing he had ever encountered.

Then he cupped his hands roughly over Sara's shoulders and pulled her close. For one scant second, she honestly thought he was going to kiss her, and she was stunned to realize she would have liked it very much if he did. But he only curled his fingers insistently into her shoulders and demanded furiously, "What the hell is going on?"

Four

Well, so much for more soft remarks about how good she smelled, Sara thought. Obviously he wanted to move on to more immediate—and more realistic—matters. Damn her luck.

"You know very well what's going on," she said, hoping she didn't sound as breathless as she felt. "We're being held hostage by a dissident group in exchange for their demands."

His grip on her shoulders tightened, and he jerked her closer still, close enough that her body was flush against his. Once again she felt the heat of him mixing with her own, only this time the sensation was compounded by the frantic beating of his heart. It mimicked the wild acceleration of her own, and Sara grew almost dizzy in response.

"That's not what I meant," he said. "I meant who the hell are you?"

Sara hesitated only a moment before replying, "You know that, too, Mr. Cordello. I'm a friend of the queen's who happens to be attending university near where you live. Her Majesty asked me if I might do her a favor and act as your escort on your journey to Penwyck. And as a loyal subject, I couldn't possibly tell her no.''

For a moment, his grip on her shoulders intensified even more. Then, suddenly, he pushed her gently away. ''Right. Escort. Whatever.''

She heard him begin to pace restlessly from one side of the tiny room to the other. ''So where do you think we are, Miss Escort?''

She answered his sarcasm with some of her own. ''Well, it appears to be a small room, doesn't it? Probably a pantry of sorts, judging by the lingering aromas of cinnamon and sage.''

''And just where is this pantry, would you say?''

''In a house, I imagine.''

He grumbled something unintelligible under his breath, something Sara was certain she was better off not hearing. ''And where do you think the house might be?'' he asked impatiently.

She sighed, losing interest in their derision. ''I'm guessing Spain, or perhaps Portugal,'' she told him. ''Though, truly, I can't be certain.''

''How long do you think we'll be here?''

Again, she answered honestly. ''I have no idea.''

''Do you think we'll survive?''

Sara straightened, stiffening her spine. ''We will if I have anything to say about it.''

The muffled voices returned then, and both Sara and Shane turned toward the door. It opened as if they'd willed it to by their simple attention, and Fawn stood framed there with a small, battery-powered flashlight, a thermos and a basket. In the light that slanted through the door from behind her, Sara saw that they were indeed in a pantry, because beyond the flight attendant was a small, tidy kitchen. Without warning, Fawn tossed the flashlight toward Sara, and, even unprepared for the gesture, she caught it quite capably. Then the other woman extended the thermos and basket to Shane, who stood nearer her.

"So you've saved me a bit of work and untied yourselves," she said. "Well done." She nodded toward Shane's burdens and added, "There's food and tea enough to get you through the night. Don't think about escaping, because you're well guarded, both inside the house and out. We've sent notice to the queen that we have you and that if she wants to see either of you again, alive and unharmed, then she'll call off the alliances with Majorco and America. With any luck, in a few days, you'll be in Penwyck. Without luck, in a few days, you'll be lying by the side of the road somewhere with bullets lodged in your brains."

And with that, she closed the door and locked it again, her footsteps fading. Sara switched on the flashlight, and was a bit surprised to find that it actually worked. She was almost sorry it did, though, when she got a good look at Shane's face in the spastic light.

Good heavens, he was angry, she thought. She told herself that his anger was directed at the Black Knights, but there was something in his look, too, that indicated at least part of his unhappiness was with her. As quickly as she had detected the anger, however, it vanished. Without even heeding what he was doing, he shoved both thermos and basket onto a shelf beside him.

"I thought you were thirsty and starved," Sara said. "Not that I wouldn't be surprised to find the provisions tainted in some way, mind you, so I can understand your reluctance."

"Thirst and hunger are the least of my worries right now," he said.

Then he covered the distance between the two of them in three long strides. She was about to take an instinctive step in retreat when he lifted his hand to her face and brushed the backs of his bent knuckles gingerly over her right—and, she knew, bruised—cheek.

"That bitch," he said in a low, menacing voice. "I can't believe I actually thought she was cute."

Somehow Sara refrained from pointing out that Fawn's thighs were much too large, and her eyebrows much too heavy, and her demeanor much too obvious for her to ever be considered cute. Instead, she only said quietly, "I'm all right."

And then somehow she did force herself to take that step in retreat. Not because she was frightened of Shane. No, she was far more fearful of the way he made her feel standing this close. The soft brush of his fingers over her skin had just been too exquisite for words.

"I've encountered worse than Fawn over the years," she added.

He grinned, but there wasn't an ounce of happiness in his expression. "Have you now?"

She nodded slowly. "I was on the girls' cricket team at school. And we were a vicious lot, I assure you."

Shane dropped his hand back to his side, and blew out an exasperated breath. "So what do we do now?"

Sara dipped her head toward the basket and thermos. "Do you want to risk eating something?"

He didn't turn his attention in that direction, but nodded. "I don't think it'll hurt us. Something tells me they don't want us dead just yet."

Oh, no, Sara agreed silently. She was sure the two of them were of much more use to the Black Knights alive. For now, at any rate.

"Then shall we?" she said.

He nodded again. "Sure. Your place or mine?"

Shane palmed his weary eyes, scrubbed his hands over his face, and wished like hell that he had access to a razor. And a sink. And a bar of soap. And—hey, why not?—a really big bottle of Scotch. He had no idea how much time had passed since he and Sara had been thrown into this little room, but they had long ago finished off the stale bread and weak tea that their captors had given them, and they'd both been allowed to take a couple of bathroom breaks. Not that knowing the time would have helped him out, anyway. He was still on Pacific Standard Time himself. His gut told him that the sun was just now rising over the east coast of the U.S.—because he was *really* in the mood for a dawn patrol surf—which would make it midafternoon where they were.

Not that he had any major plans for the day or any important appointments he had to keep. So what was the big deal, right?

He told himself he should try to get some sleep, that he was useless to himself and Sara in his current state of exhaustion. Although he'd nodded off once or twice since they'd eaten, he hadn't been able to do anything more than doze intermittently. He supposed he was still a little buzzed over all the adrenaline that had pumped through his body in the last few days, ever since receiving that fateful phone call from Marcus and the queen of Penwyck. Between that and this little episode with the Black Knights, his body and mind both were on overload. He guessed he shouldn't be surprised that sleep eluded him.

He glanced over at his companion to find that she suffered from no such problem herself. In fact, Sara had succumbed to her own exhaustion and fallen into a deep sleep a long time ago—though he wasn't sure exactly how long. Hell, he couldn't be sure about much of anything at this point. Except for the fact that Sara Wallington looked pretty damned adorable when she slept.

Her pink sweater and white blouse were smudged with dirt and dust in a number of places now, and her crisp tailored skirt was more than a little sooty and rumpled. Her stockings bore a long run in one of the legs, and the hijackers had taken her shoes along with his own. Her hair had long ago spilled from its terse binding, and now it cascaded in a tangle over her shoulders and forehead. He'd been surprised to see that it was slightly curly, so tightly had she had it bound. Even the shiner she sported courtesy of Fawn the Terrible couldn't harden her appearance. She was still Miss Pink Sweater and Pearls, even if the terrorists had swiped her pearls along with her shoes.

Still, there was something about her current state of disorder that made Shane smile, because it hinted at a rash, untamed nature that might lurk beneath her carefully created, pink-sweatered exterior. And even though she'd been through hell, she'd managed to hang on to her spirit and her courage and her dignity. She might be pink sweaters and pearls, but there was steel and fire beneath them. And all Shane could think about at the moment was what an appealing bundle of contradictions she was, and about how very much he wanted to wake her up and make love to her right here.

Whoa. Hold on thar, Babalooie. Make love? To Miss Pink Sweater? Was he crazy?

It was the weirdest damned thing he'd ever thought. Here he was, in a situation that defied reality, his life hanging in the balance, and suddenly he wanted to make love to a woman he'd met only a couple of days ago. Certainly an immediate physical response to a woman wasn't exactly uncharacteristic behavior for Shane. But it *was* unusual for him to want a woman with the vigor that he wanted Sara at that moment.

He told himself he shouldn't be surprised by the intensity of his response, and that it was the very nature of their bizarre circumstances that probably generated it. Hadn't he read somewhere that being in a dangerous situation heightened a person's awareness and created an artificial sort of intimacy with anyone else who might be caught up in the perilous doings? So of course he shouldn't be surprised by his reaction to Sara right now. But he was. Even danger and peril shouldn't make him feel this way about a woman. Especially a woman like her. Because, in spite of the steel and fire, she was much too decent and much too sweet for the kind of thoughts he was having about her.

Even if she was lying about who she was.

Oh, he didn't doubt she was a student. She was much too…too…too *studious* not to be. But she for sure wasn't majoring in English or home ec or library science, as he had originally supposed. Not unless it was a front for something else. He just wished he knew who and what she was and why she was misleading him.

He shoved his fingers vigorously through his hair again, as if he were trying to literally push the troubling thoughts out of his brain. Man, he was tired. He couldn't remember a time when he'd felt this exhausted, not even when he'd pulled a double shift hauling bricks after a day-long surfing tourney last year. He closed his eyes, thinking maybe if he just sat still enough, cleared his mind enough, he might fall into the same kind of deep slumber that Sara had fallen into.

No sooner had the thought unrolled in his head, however, than he heard her stirring on the other side of the tiny room. When he opened his eyes again, in the weakening light of the flashlight, he saw her push herself into a sitting position. She groaned as she extended her arms outward and launched herself into a stout stretch, and Shane tried not to notice how the action thrust her breasts against the thin white cotton of her shirt, tried not to think about how the sound she made was so like the one a woman uttered when she was thoroughly—sexually—satisfied.

For a moment, she seemed not to remember that he was there, probably didn't even recall the details of her current predicament. She looked like a woman just waking from a long sleep, and Shane was reluctant to say anything to hurry her awareness. Hell, she deserved a few moments of forgetfulness when the reality to which she would finally awaken was so awful. So he only watched in silence as she pushed her arms over her head, then folded them behind her neck for another long stretch. The top button of her blouse freed itself when she did, revealing the merest hint of pale pink lace and ivory flesh beneath. And just like that,

Shane went hard as a rock with his need to have her *right now*.

Dammit. That was the *last* thing he needed right now.

But he couldn't take his eyes off of her as, with one final flexing of her fingers and one last lusty sigh, she eased herself out of her stretch. Slowly, she curled her legs behind herself and dropped her arms to her sides, leaning back on one hand as she settled the other in her lap. She rolled her head back and forth a time or two, then finally opened her eyes—her bewitching pale green eyes—and turned her gaze to Shane. Immediately, those eyes went wide, and he realized she had indeed, until that moment, forgotten where she was and what had been happening.

And then, as if to illustrate, she said softly, "Damn. I was so hoping I'd only dreamed all that."

He smiled halfheartedly at the way she swore in such a dignified, rarefied voice, then murmured, "Hey, welcome to my nightmare."

She expelled a reluctant chuckle. "You mean *our* nightmare."

"Well, I guess I don't mind sharing it," he said. "If you insist."

She sighed wearily and cast her gaze around their meager prison. "Doesn't look as if we have much choice, does it?"

Man, he was loving her voice, loving the dulcet, cultivated accent and the soft pitch, and the way her tone went down at the end of a question instead of up. It was just so different from the way he talked himself, and so incredibly sexy. Especially now, because her voice sounded so refined while the rest of her looked so reckless. And now, with her looking the way she did and sounding the way she did...

Don't think about it, Cordello. Just forget all about that stuff.

Of course, forgetting about all that stuff was going to be just a *tad* difficult for him to manage, seeing as how he was trapped with her indefinitely, in a room that was barely big enough for one person, let alone two. And seeing as how she kept talking in that incredibly sexy voice. And seeing as how she looked all rumpled and adorable and sexy. And seeing as how the top button on her blouse was still unbuttoned and still hinting—sexily—at the pale pink lace and ivory flesh beneath.

Shane stifled an inward groan and squeezed his eyes shut tight.

"I say, I do feel a bit better for having slept," he heard Sara say in that refined, reckless—sexy—voice.

Well, that makes one of us, he thought.

"Did you manage to get any yourself?" she added.

Did he get any? Oh, now there was a loaded question.

"Sleep, I mean."

Oh, that. Not in this lifetime or any other.

"You'd feel better if you could."

And I'd feel even better if I...and you...could— Enough, Cordello!

He forced his eyes open again, but alas, Sara Wallington still looked way too sexy for his comfort. Worse than that, she was gazing back at him as if she expected him to do something. Something like, oh... Shane didn't know. Maybe crawl over to her side of the cramped space and pull her into his arms and cover her mouth with his and—

"Did you hear the Black Knights say anything while I was sleeping?" she asked. "Did they do anything I should know about?"

Oh, excellent, he thought. Way to go, Sara. Talking about their current predicament was as successful as having a bucket of ice water tossed in his face—or elsewhere—in cooling his ardor.

He shook his head. "Nada," he told her, still trying not to notice that unbuttoned button. "I haven't heard a thing. No movement, no talking, nothing. They might as well be sleeping themselves."

She studied him intently for a moment. "I suppose they do need to sleep, as well, don't they?"

"Yeah, but it's not likely they'll do it while they're on

watch. And anyway, I figure it's probably afternoon now, local time.''

"Yes, it is," she said readily.

Her quick agreement surprised him. "How can you tell?"

She shrugged. "I just can, that's all. As you said, though," she hastily backtracked, "none of them would be sleeping on watch, regardless of the time, would they? Still..."

Her voice trailed off, as if she were thinking about something, though Shane was pretty sure her thoughts didn't run along the same lines his had been running along. His suspicion was confirmed when she added softly, "We'll have to figure out some way to escape, of course."

He expelled an incredulous sound at that. "And how are we supposed to do that? Not only do they outnumber us, but they're armed. They're also the ones with the keys to the doors and the car. Not to mention we have no idea where we are, and are therefore at a slight disadvantage. I mean, hell, even if we get out of the house—which isn't likely—how do we know which way is the right way? We could end up in an even worse situation than this. And what if we don't speak the language? How are we supposed to get someone to help us?"

"I speak the language, regardless of what it is," she assured him. "Have no fear there." Her voice hardened and her expression grew grave as she added, "And trust me, Mr. Cordello, when I tell you that a worse situation than this probably isn't possible."

For a long time, he only gazed at her in silence, wondering what she knew that he didn't know, and how she could know it so well. Then, softly, "Shane," he finally said.

She narrowed her eyes at him curiously. "I beg your pardon?"

"Enough of the 'Mr. Cordello' stuff. My name is Shane.

You've called me that once. There's no reason for you to go back to formalities.''

Except, he thought, that formalities might be a good idea, considering how *in*formal his thoughts about her were becoming.

''Fine,'' she replied. ''And, of course, you must call me Sara.''

''Is that an order, General Wallington?''

She smiled. ''Yes, I suppose it is.''

Neither seemed to know what to say after that, leading to a long silence that seemed to want to stretch on to forever. Before it could get too awkward, Shane said the first thing that came into his head. ''So how did you become so militant, anyway? Is your father in the Penwyck Royal Navy or something?''

She smiled cryptically…and, he thought, a little sadly for some reason. ''He *was* in something like that, yes.''

''Army?'' Shane said.

''Not exactly.''

''Air force?''

''No.''

''Marines?''

''Afraid not.''

''Then what?''

She turned away, her smile now seeming nervous somehow. ''My father worked for the government,'' she said evasively.

''And you're following in his footsteps?''

''You could say that.''

''Ambassador?''

''Of sorts.''

Shane gritted his teeth. ''Why don't you like to talk about yourself? What are you trying to hide?''

She shrugged, steering her gaze at some point behind Shane, but there was nothing casual in her posture at all. ''I'm not trying to hide anything,'' she told him. ''There's just nothing to tell, that's all. I've led a very boring life, I assure you."

"I bet there's plenty to tell," Shane countered. "I bet your life has been fascinating."

"Well, you'd lose both bets. My life has been utterly uneventful."

"Until now," he pointed out.

This time, when she replied, she looked him square in the eye. "Until now, yes."

"So how did you get to this point, hmm?" he asked.

"Probably the same way you did. Wrong place, wrong time."

Shane shook his head decisively. "No. Something tells me you were right where you were supposed to be, at exactly the right time. There's something going on here that you're not telling me, but I'm damned if I know what. Something you're involved in that you don't want me to know about for some reason."

She expelled another one of those anxious chuckles. "What a vivid imagination you've got."

He grinned knowingly. "Yeah, haven't I, though?"

Hastily, she changed the subject. "How about you, Mr. Cordello?"

"Shane," he corrected her.

"Yes, of course. How about you?"

He noticed she didn't speak his given name. Again. Apparently, she couldn't do that when the situation was less volatile. Or maybe when the situation was more intimate. Interesting, that. "What about me?"

"What's brought you to this point?"

"A hijacking," he replied succinctly.

"You know what I meant," she countered.

"Not really," he said. He smiled again, surprised to realize that it felt like the flirtatious one he only used with women he was trying to lure into bed. Okay, so maybe that wasn't so surprising, after all, all things considered. "Not unless you're just trying to get to know me better."

She shrugged. "Well, it's not like we have anything better to do with our time, is it?"

And, oh, put like that, didn't it sound as if she was just *so* interested in getting to know him better? Shane thought wryly.

"We could play Twenty Questions," he suggested. Suggestively, he hoped, because on top of all the other erratic—erotic—thoughts he'd been having about Miss Sara Wallington, he hadn't quite been able to banish the memory of how she had been looking at him just before they were hijacked and kidnapped. "We never did get to play our game before. We were rather rudely interrupted."

"Mmm," she replied noncommittally. "Strangely, this isn't normally how things turn out when I meet a man for the first time."

"You don't say," Shane replied, feeling surprisingly playful now. "What does normally happen when you meet a man for the first time?"

She lifted one shoulder and let it drop, an action that made her blouse gape open a bit more, enough for Shane to get more of a maddening glimpse of the lacy bra and soft skin beneath. He bit back a groan and tried very, very hard not to notice. Honest, he did. Really.

"We usually go to dinner and a movie," she said. "Or, if I like a man very much, we go dancing."

"And then?"

"And then I let him walk me home."

"And then?"

"And then what?" she asked, looking genuinely puzzled.

"Do you invite him in?"

She gaped softly. "Of course not. Not on the first date."

"Not even for a nightcap?"

"Certainly not," she answered crisply.

"Like to play hard to get, do you?"

She leveled a steady gaze on him. "I assure you, Mr. Cordello, there is no playing involved. I *am* hard to get."

"Shane," he said again. "You're supposed to call me Shane."

And of course she was hard to get, he thought. That was what was going to make having her all the more fun, once he caught her. Because he knew in that moment that he *was* going to catch Sara Wallington. Better still, he was going to *have* her. Eventually. Once they got out of this predicament. And they *would* get out of this predicament, he thought further. Eventually.

"Ah, yes," she said, bringing him back to the present. "So I am."

But so she wasn't, he couldn't help noting. Again. "It's interesting that you keep forgetting to call me by my first name," he said.

"Is it?"

"I think so."

"Mmm," she said again. But she offered no further clarification.

Another one of those awkward silences threatened to follow, so Shane hastily tried again. "So," he said, "you want to try again?"

"Try what again?"

"Twenty Questions. Because I'm thinking of something *really* good right now." He tried really hard not to leer as he added, "And I bet you could guess what it is in a lot less than twenty questions."

Five

Sara shook her head in response to Shane's suggestive suggestion. "I'd much rather hear about you and your brother, Marcus," she told him. "One of you may, after all, be the next reigning king of my homeland. It isn't every day a woman is presented with an opportunity like this."

And oh, wasn't *that* just the biggest understatement she had ever uttered in her life, Sara thought as she studied him more resolutely. He looked like hell, all scruffy and unshaven and exhausted. His blue eyes were smudged by shadows beneath, and his shaggy brown hair was shaggier than ever, falling over his forehead and nearly into his eyes, giving him the appearance of some menacing highwayman.

At some point, he'd torn a hole in his jeans, a straight slash across the right leg that left his knee exposed when he bent it to make himself more comfortable. His white T-shirt was looking a bit rumpled beneath his jean jacket, but it still hugged his lean, muscular frame like a lover's embrace. And he had a hole in one sock, she further noted with a smile, something that made him incredibly endearing somehow, as if he needed someone to take care of him, because he couldn't even manage his socks.

Not that she saw *herself* as a candidate for caretaker, mind you. Sara had no desire to care for anyone except herself. And not that Shane Cordello needed to be made any more endearing to her than he was already. Because even looking like hell, he was somehow infinitely more appealing to her than any man she had ever met. Too appealing, she realized. Because ever since waking from her nap, she'd been *much* too aware of his presence. Worse, he was present in a way that men simply were not present with her. Certainly not this soon after meeting one. In fact, she couldn't think of a single man of her acquaintance who had captivated her as quickly and as thoroughly as Shane had.

Oh, dear. This *really* wasn't a good time for that.

"Tell you what," he said, scattering her thoughts. "I'll answer your questions about me and Marcus if you'll answer my questions about you. Ten questions each," he added. "That'll be twenty questions."

"All right," she told him. "Sounds fair."

"You go first," he said.

She eyed him intently as her questions about him tumbled through her brain—for truly, it was Shane she most wanted to learn about, and not his brother, Marcus—and she tried to decide which one to ask first. Finally, what she settled on was "Where did you go to college?"

"UCLA," he replied promptly.

"And what was your major?"

He grinned cockily. "Girls."

She muttered a soft *tsk* before pointing out, "That's not a major."

"Not an officially sanctioned one, maybe, but it *is* a major. And with *a lot* of college guys, too."

"And did you earn your degree in this major?" Sara asked saucily.

"Whoa, yeah," he replied with a chuckle that bordered on arrogant.

Sara couldn't help laughing, too. "What was your minor then?"

"Goofing off," he said. "Aced that one, too," he added proudly.

"And what was your paper degree in?" she asked more pointedly. "Can you even remember?"

"That one I had a little trouble earning," Shane said without a trace of apology. "Never did get it."

"Why not?"

He shrugged. "I wasn't the college type."

"But why not?" she asked again.

Another shrug. "I didn't take well to sitting in classes all day. I wanted to be outside. Wanted to be *doing* something."

"You don't think studying is doing?"

"For some people it is," he conceded. "But not for me. I like working with my hands. And I like fresh air."

"So you dropped out?"

He nodded. "In my third year. I got a job pouring cement on a construction site and, after a while, I worked my way up to foreman. I like what I do," he added adamantly, as if it were very important that she understand that. "I'm proud of my work." Then, "That's ten questions," he told her. "My turn."

"That wasn't ten," she immediately contradicted him.

"Yeah, it was."

"No, it wasn't."

He held up one hand as he began to enumerate. "Where'd I go to college, my major, my minor, my paper degree and a bunch of 'Why nots' and stuff in between. Ten total."

"You can't count the 'why nots,'" Sara told him.

"Why not?"

"Because they're not real questions."

"They have question marks at the end."

"Yes, but—"

"That makes them questions."

"But—"

"So now it's my turn, and here's my first question for you." He pointed a finger toward her abdomen as he asked, "Did you know your shirt's unbuttoned?"

It took a few moments for Sara to realize a few things. Number one, that he had turned the tables on her so smoothly and so completely. Number two, that he had, in fact, asked the question that he had asked. And number three, whether or not he had been serious in asking the question. That in itself branched off into a couple of other moments, as she first had to glance down at the garment he indicated to see if the question actually applied—it did, unfortunately—and then she had to decide whether or not the question was an appropriate one for him *to* ask. It wasn't, not for mixed company. Of course, their present situation being a bit, oh, bizarre, she supposed it was all right to make allowances.

But still.

When her brain *finally* stopped buzzing with all its strange musings, Sara hastily lifted a hand to her blouse and fastened not just the button to which Shane had referred, but every other button, as well, until her collar nearly strangled her in its closeness. She heard him chuckling as she completed the action, and she supposed it *was* a bit late for modesty at this point, but she couldn't quite bring herself to undo what she had done. All she could do was glance up again to see him sitting on the other side of the room, his elbow propped on one bent knee, his fingers curled loosely over his mouth, laughing at her.

"Is there something you find humorous, Mr. Cordello?" she asked.

He dropped his hand from his mouth, but still folded it arrogantly over his knee, and grinned devilishly. "You know, I don't have to answer that question, because it's number eleven."

"I've stopped playing," she said crisply.

"Have you? Really?"

"That's three questions you've asked now," she pointed out before she could stop herself.

He laughed again. "So you *are* still playing," he said smugly. "Thanks for answering my questions, even if I had to infer your answers, because you didn't really answer, and even if you did, it was really only one answer for two questions, which means, if I wanted to, I could disqualify those answers—and therefore those questions—and ask you another question or two instead. But I won't do that," he told her magnanimously. "Because, hey, that's just the kind of guy I am."

In response to his assertion—or whatever all those words strung together had been—all Sara could manage was an impatient expulsion of air, followed by a softly muttered "Oh, please."

Shane didn't seem put off by her reply, however, because his pompous expression grew even more arrogant. For a moment, he only gazed at her in silence. Then he must have been struck by something, because he heaved himself over onto all fours and began to crawl slowly—intently—across the few feet of flooring that separated them.

For some reason, watching him approach her in such a way made Sara feel as if she had become some small prey who was caught in the hypnotic glower of a fierce predator. Try as she might to make herself move—or even to make herself look away, to break that hypnosis—she couldn't budge. Not that there was anywhere for her to go, she reminded herself. But she didn't have to just sit there, gazing back at him, as if she were completely under his spell, did she? She wasn't defenseless, after all. Well, not normally. With Shane drawing nearer, however, she suddenly felt as if she hadn't a grain of self-preservation left inside her.

And then he was right beside her, seating himself as close to her as he could without actually touching her. And although the last thing she needed or wanted at that moment was to be touched by Shane, she was oddly disappointed that he left even an infinitesimal amount of space between them. Until he leaned forward, very nearly touching her, the heat of his body mingling with her own. Until, with his mouth dangerously close to her ear, he murmured, very softly, "Please what?"

The words were warm and damp against her face, and an equally warm, damp sensation meandered through Sara at hearing them. "I...I...I don't know...what you...what you mean," she stammered, her own voice a scant whisper.

He didn't move an inch, neither forward nor back, and his breath was torrid against her neck when he replied, as softly as before, "You said, 'Oh, please.' And I was wondering what you were saying 'please' for. I mean, if you're asking what I think you are, believe me, Sara, you don't have to ask politely. You don't have to say, 'please.' In fact," he continued in that same sweltering, seductive voice, leaning so close now that she fancied she could actually feel his mouth caressing her ear oh so very softly, "in fact, you don't have to ask at all."

What little air was left in her lungs suddenly left her in a quick, quiet *whoosh*. Her mouth went dry, her throat constricted and every cell in her body flared with a need and a hunger unlike any she had ever known. *Need*, she then mimicked to herself. *Hunger*. What common little words those were for what she was feeling in that moment. *Urgency* was more like it. Or *craving*. Because suddenly Sara felt as if she couldn't make it through another moment of her life without having Shane touch her. Pull her close. Kiss her. Make love to her.

Her response made no sense. Sara had never felt a need or a hunger for any man, and certainly not an urgency or craving. It was why she was still untutored in the actual mechanics of lovemaking. Oh, she knew what went on between a man and a woman when they wanted each other, to be sure. But she'd never felt compelled to explore the activity herself. She had no moral or social objection to premarital sex—she'd simply never met a man who'd made her *want* to have sex, any more than she'd met a man who'd made her entertain the possibility of marriage. Simply put, Sara didn't want to be married at this point in her life, and she didn't want to be sexually involved. So she wasn't. And she was far too pragmatic a person to offer herself up to the likeliest candidate for her deflowering just because she was old enough, or mature enough, or whatever enough, to do it.

Besides, her studies had always come first. As did planning for her career that would follow. She'd had boyfriends in the past, certainly. But none of them had meant enough to her to make her feel as if she wanted to surrender—everything—to them.

Shane Cordello did, though.

In one scant instant, just by his nearness and a few softly uttered words, he made her want to give him all of those things that she had kept to herself for so long now. He made her want to abandon everything except him and the way he made her feel, made her want to forget all about her studies, her career, her family, their current state of captivity…

Oh, God, their current state of captivity! How in heaven's name could she have forgotten *that?*

Hastily, she pushed herself sideways, away from Shane, until a good foot of space separated them. Only then was she able to breathe again. Only then was she able to think clearly again. Only then could she remind herself that this was *not* the place to fall in love, and Shane was *not* the kind of man to fall in—

Oh, no, no, no, no, no, Sara, she halted herself frantically. *Watch how you choose your words.*

Love had nothing to do with any of this. What she was experiencing was a simple by-product of a stressful, threatening situation. Every instinct she had was on overdrive due to her present circumstances, her sexual ones right up there with her survival ones. Her response to Shane was purely physical, she told herself. Utterly chemical. There was nothing emotional about it. Nothing.

She heard him chuckle low again, and snapped her head around to look at him. "What's so funny?" she asked.

But he only chuckled harder in response. "You know, you really don't play this game fairly at all," he said. "Because you keep asking questions, even though your turn was up a long time ago."

Sara bit back a growl. "Fine," she bit off roughly. "Then ask your bloody questions so I can have a turn again. You have six left."

He opened his mouth as if he intended to contradict her, but something in her expression must have made him reconsider, because he only grinned that maddeningly smug grin again and nodded. "Okay," he said, "number five." He hesitated before asking it, however, eyeing her with much speculation, evidently giving the question much thought before speaking it. Finally, though, he asked, "What's your major?"

"Well, it isn't boys," she replied coolly.

"That I could tell."

"Not that I couldn't graduate with highest honors there if I wanted to," she felt compelled to add. Probably because of the bland expression on his face that seemed to challenge her for some reason.

"Hey, I don't doubt that for a moment," he assured her.

She strove for a jesting smile that somehow didn't feel any more convincing than it probably looked. "Actually, if I tell you my major, I'll have to kill you," she quipped.

Shane glanced first left, and then right, then met her gaze levelly once again. "Gee, forgive me if I don't take the threat all that seriously. You might have noticed that I'm already kind of in dire straits here."

Sara expelled a soft sound of resolution. She might as well tell him the truth. It wasn't any big secret, really, not her studies. Someday the career she intended to undertake would be very hush-hush and mysterious, but there were no hard-and-fast rules about her university studies. Besides, there was still a good chance neither of them would make it out of this thing alive, making anything they said or did to each other completely irrelevant. At least to outward appearances.

"I suppose you could say my major is political science," she began.

"Could I?"

She nodded. "Specifically, my studies focus on counterterrorism."

"Which is why you know so much about the Black Knights."

"Actually, no," Sara said. "Them I was already an expert on when I chose my field of study."

"Oh, yeah?"

She nodded. "Yes. You see, they murdered my father. He was killed by a bomb they planted at the RII offices eight years ago."

The only reaction Shane showed to her announcement was to let his mouth fall slightly open. But his eyes seemed to grow darker somehow, colder, stormier. And his entire body seemed to go rigid, though Sara saw no actual tensing of his muscles. It was just that, one moment, he seemed relaxed and jovial and eager to tease, and the next moment, he seemed poised for attack. Attack on whom, however, Sara couldn't say for sure. But suddenly he looked like a man who wanted to hit something. Or someone. Very badly indeed.

"Okay, next question," he said, his voice low and gritty and menacing. "What's the RII?"

"The Royal Intelligence Institute," Sara clarified. "They're a government agency that act as the king's right-hand men and women, so to speak. My father worked for them."

She didn't go into further detail, and Shane didn't seem to want any. Not about the RII, at any rate. Because his next question was, "And just who the hell are the Black Knights?"

As questions went, Sara thought, that one pretty much used up every one Shane had left, and she told him so.

"I don't care," he replied. "I think it's about time you told me exactly what we're up against, Sara. Obviously these guys haven't had any kind of response to their demands, or else we wouldn't be sitting here having this conversation."

"No," she agreed, "I imagine we'd be dead."

His expression hardened even more, something she wouldn't have thought possible. "All the more reason for you to give me the whole story," he said. "I think I deserve to know exactly what we're up against."

He was right, of course. In fact, he was long past due being told as much about their situation as she knew herself. They'd been sitting here long enough for the Black Knights to have made their demands known to Queen Marissa. But if Sara knew the queen—and, of course, she did—then Her Majesty was doing everything she could to stall, in an effort to buy some time and organize the Royal Intelligence Institute, so that they could find and free her and Shane. Unfortunately, Sara also knew the Black Knights. And there was a very good chance indeed that the RII wouldn't reach the captives before they met with a bad end.

"As I told you before," she began in her most professional voice, trying not to think about that last bit for now, "the Black Knights have been around for about a decade. These days, they're a sinister lot, to be sure, very well organized and very well funded, and completely without morals or scruples. Who's doing the funding, no one knows for certain, in spite of extensive investigation. Theories abound, however, and some of them even point rather high in the Penwyck administration. There are even some who think—"

Here, Sara halted. Shane didn't need an advanced course

in the Black Knights. What he needed was the introductory version. Not only were there facts and theories about the group that weren't relative to their current situation, but knowing too much could honestly be dangerous for him.

She started again. "Anyway, no one can say exactly for sure who runs the organization, and we've not been able to identify where their financing comes from. But this past year alone, they've been responsible for a number of acts of sabotage against both the military and the government, not to mention the kidnapping of Prince Owen and the attempted kidnapping of Princess Anastasia."

At this, Shane's head snapped up. "What? No one told me anything about any kidnappings."

"Well, Owen and Anastasia both were eventually safely recovered, and the kidnapping of her children isn't exactly the kind of thing Her Majesty wants to dwell on, is it? But it's not been any great secret." She shook her head slowly again. "All in all, it's been an odd year for the royal family, I'm afraid. The queen found out her brother was involved in an assassination attempt on the king some years back. Princess Anastasia had a bout with amnesia, of all things. Princess Meredith took ill and there was concern she would lose her baby. Owen found out he fathered a child four years ago, while he was in America at school. And Princess Megan turned up pregnant, out of wedlock, which was scandalous enough in itself. Of course, she eventually married the baby's father, but he's the earl of Silvershire, of all things, which goes beyond scandal."

"Uh, why is that such a bad thing?" Shane asked.

"Well, he's from Drogheda, for heaven's sake," she said, certain that would be the only comment necessary there.

Shane, however, didn't seem to understand. "And that would be significant because...?" he asked.

Sara expelled an impatient sound. She didn't have time to tell him the history of the warring nations of Penwyck and Drogheda. Instead, she only told him, "Well, the families have been feuding for generations, haven't they? The last thing anyone could have seen coming was a royal wedding uniting them.''

''Ah,'' he said, though he clearly didn't understand at all.

So Sara continued as best she could. ''But as strange as all those developments are, none of them is the strangest thing that's happened in Penwyck. The strangest thing is that King Morgan contracted viral encephalitis and lapsed into a coma around the time of the wedding—something else we suspect the Black Knights are behind—and the RII trotted out his identical twin to rule the country in his place. They're quite a powerful group, and they stepped in when the king went into his coma. Thing is, though, the RII never bothered to tell anyone at first, not even the queen, that it was Broderick they'd put in charge, and not King Morgan—''

''Broderick?''

''The king's twin,'' Sara clarified. ''Evil twin if you ask me, though no one wanted my opinion, did they?''

''I don't know. Did they?''

''Well, no one asked.''

''Mmm,'' Shane replied blandly. But his expression, one of mild humor, told her she was revealing too much of the personal now, which wouldn't be tolerated by the RII once—if—she landed a job with them.

''Anyway,'' she continued, doing her best to curb her opinions, ''Broderick's been running Penwyck in the king's place, and mucking things up royally, if you ask me.'' All right, so maybe she wasn't doing her *very* best to curb her opinions. ''And now there's this mix-up with the princes where, technically, there could be four of you to choose from for running the country. It's like a bad soap opera, honestly.''

''Three,'' Shane corrected her.

''Well, yes, I suppose there is enough going on for three soap operas, now that I think about it,'' Sara agreed.

"No, I didn't mean three soap operas," he said. "I meant three to choose from for running the country."

"What?" she asked.

"Three to choose from," he repeated. "I'm not running any country."

She gaped at him, not sure what to make of his assertion. "But what if you're next in line for the Penwyck throne?"

"In the first place," Shane said, "that isn't likely, because I find it very hard to believe that Marcus and I were switched at birth with anyone. Hell, I still can't make myself believe we were adopted. In the second place, Marcus is older than me by almost thirty minutes, so even if we did end up being the missing heirs to the throne, he has seniority over me, being firstborn and all. Plus, he's been heading up an international financial empire for years now, so ruling a small sovereign nation should be a piece of cake for him. And in the third place, even if they offered the job to me, I don't want it."

This, Sara thought, was quite a surprise. Oh, certainly Shane Cordello made it clear that he was his own man who lived by his own rules, but she couldn't imagine any man turning down the position of king of his own country, no matter what.

"You say that now," Sara said, "but you'd feel differently if someone actually told you that you're next in line to be king of Penwyck."

Shane shook his head. "No, I say that no matter what. I don't want to be king of anything."

"Rubbish," she said before she could stop herself. "Every man wants to be king of something. It's all about control with you."

He looked taken aback by her statement, and only then did she realize how vehemently—and revealingly—she had spoken.

"Well, my, my, my," he said softly. "Haven't we just hit a raw nerve with General Wallington?"

Sara closed her eyes for a moment, counted slowly to

five, then opened them again. "All right," she conceded, "I'll grant you that you did in fact touch a bit of a sore spot with me on that one."

"Why?"

"Why is not important," she assured him. Well, it wasn't important to Shane Cordello, at any rate, she told herself. "And perhaps I was a bit overly sweeping in my observation," she further conceded. "However," she added quickly when she saw him open his mouth to object, "I still say that most men, if given the opportunity, would jump at the chance to be king of their own country. And yes, with many of them, it is most definitely a control issue."

He eyed her levelly for a moment, his gaze so focused and so intense, it made her want to squirm. Then, very quietly, very evenly, he told her, "I'm not most men, Sara. I'm not even many of them."

Well, that, of course, was something she had noticed about him some time ago. Though not, probably, in the way he meant. "But we digress," she continued, less zealously this time.

"Right," he agreed. "We were talking about why you think men are control freaks."

"No, we were talking about all the strange things going on with the royal family," she corrected him smoothly.

"Oh, yeah. We can talk about the control thing later."

Not. Bloody. Likely, Sara thought. Before she had a chance to say anything, however—not that she was going to say *that*, of course—Shane continued speaking.

"Why wasn't I told about any of this before now?" he asked.

Sara blew out a weary breath and wondered that herself. "Well, perhaps Her Majesty thought you wouldn't come to Penwyck if you knew the current climate of the country and royal family."

"Perhaps Her Majesty was right," he replied dryly.

"I'm sure she planned to tell you everything once you arrived. This trip was rather hastily put together, after all."

"Yeah, and look what happens when you fly by night like that," he quipped. Then he blew out an exasperated breath and shook his head slowly. "I have *got* to start watching the evening news more often."

"Not that the American news channels much cover what happens in Penwyck," Sara reminded him. "The best news I receive of home is what I get from my mother and sisters. You shouldn't feel badly about not knowing. You know now."

"But what I know answers very few of my questions," he said. "I mean, what was all that business about diamonds on the plane? Fawn said something about diamonds, and then one of the other guys shut her up. Fast. What was she talking about?"

"I have no idea," Sara replied honestly. "I assumed they kidnapped you because of your possible tie to the throne, and your value there. They've already kidnapped and released Prince Owen. Perhaps they know something we don't. Perhaps Owen *isn't* in line to the throne and you *are,* which would put them in a very good bargaining position indeed. But diamonds?" she asked, genuinely puzzled. "I can't imagine where they fit in. It's the alliances with Majorco and America they seem most concerned about. Of course—"

She had been about to say that of course, there was quite a lot to which she wasn't privy, so her having heard nothing was meaningless. She wasn't a member of the RII and wouldn't be until she graduated, though she'd been all but promised a job there once she did complete her studies. Still, of course she wouldn't know about the workings of the elite spy network that answered to the king and queen until she was one of them. Even then, it would be a long time before she was put to work on anything of significance—like the Black Knights. First she'd have to prove herself in the field like all the other newly hired operatives.

Even if her father had been a well-respected member of the group at one time.

"But the Black Knights are clearly up to something," she finally concluded. "And trust me, Shane, when I tell you that they really will stop at nothing to meet their needs. They truly are a sinister lot, and we'd be best off assuming the worst from them."

"Then we need to get out of here," he said. "As soon as possible."

"Yes, of course," Sara said. "I'll just ring up Queen Marissa on my cell phone and have her send round a car, shall I? Perhaps they can stop at the local market for sandwiches on their way."

Shane threw her a sarcastic look. "I didn't say it would be easy."

"No, you didn't say much of anything," she pointed out. "But if you have a better plan, I'd very much like to hear it."

He smiled a deliberate, menacing smile. "Oh, I have a plan," he told her. "In fact, I have an *ex*cellent plan."

Six

He was probably going to get them both killed, Shane thought some time later. But, hell, Sara had agreed to go along with his plan, so she'd be equally responsible for their deaths, wouldn't she?

Strangely, the realization did nothing to comfort him.

But as they sat in the darkness—the batteries of the flashlight burned out—waiting for the arrival of something or someone, he couldn't help second-guessing himself. He told himself that they didn't have any choice but to attempt an escape. There was no guarantee that the Black Knights would let them live, even if Queen Marissa did meet their demands. In fact, if what Sara said was true—and he had no reason to doubt her—the opposite was more likely, and the Black Knights would kill them, whether their demands were met or not.

So their only alternative, clearly, was to escape. If they could. Shane just hoped they were both strong enough, and brave enough—and lucky enough—to manage it.

The time for finding out whether or not they were came more quickly than he had thought—or hoped—it would. Because no sooner had that last thought formed in his brain than he heard the sound of approaching footsteps. It had been a while since any of the kidnappers had checked on them, and he assumed they must be bringing another meal. Instead, he hoped, they were offering them another bathroom break, because they really needed to get out of this room if they were going to have any chance of success. It would be even more helpful if only one of the Black Knights came to the door. It would be most helpful of all if it was Fawn. Because, hey, she fought like a girl.

Of course, so did Sara, Shane reminded himself, and she was pretty damned formidable. Still, Sara fought with a cool, calm head, and Fawn was easily provoked to do something rash, as he'd seen for himself on the plane. He'd place his bet on Sara in a heartbeat.

The gods must have heard his pleas and prayers, because when the door to the pantry/prison opened, it was indeed Fawn who stood there. She held the basket and thermos again—which one of the men had collected when two of them had come to release Shane and Sara for their earlier bathroom breaks, so it must be dinnertime now. Fawn was looking a little more fatigued and strained than she had looked earlier that day, and Shane couldn't help wondering if she was having as much trouble sleeping as he was.

Before any of them could say a word, however Shane heard a sound outside and tuned his ear to listen more closely. And when he realized what the sound was, he had to bite back a grin at just how wonderful it was to hear. In fact, it was the sweetest sound he had ever heard in his entire life—better than the roar of the ocean as it curled over him while he was surfing, better than the sizzle of a fat sausage on the grill, better even, than the breathy murmur of a well-satisfied woman when she woke next to him on a balmy Sunday morning.

Because what Shane heard was the sound of a car driving away.

At least one of the kidnappers had left the house. With any luck at all, two had gone. That would leave two there with him and Sara, evening the odds nicely. Even if three remained, they were still better off. He glanced over at Sara to see if she'd noticed the sound, too, and saw immediately by her jubilant expression that she had. Then, pretending he hadn't heard anything at all, he focused his attention on Fawn.

"Can I use the bathroom?" he said without preamble.

She widened her eyes in surprise. "But it's not time for that."

"Yeah, well, the call of nature and all that, honey," he said. "Man's gotta do what a man's gotta do." He threw her what he'd been told was his most winning smile, even though winning Fawn was about as appealing as winning a cold sore. "To put it in the vernacular," he added, oozing as much boyish charm as he could, and trying not to gag on it, "I gotta use the can."

"But it's not time for that," she said again. "It's time for you to eat. You can use the washroom later."

Instead of replying this time, Shane stood—slowly, cautiously, with his arms extended at his sides, so that she wouldn't think he was trying to pull anything funny. Ha.

"Look, Fawn," he began again, keeping his voice courteous, and trying not to be too smarmy, "I'm just not as used to downing that tea as you Penwyckians are, and trust me when I tell you that if you don't let me out of here to go to the bathroom, I'm going to get very…frustrated."

Fawn expelled a long, ragged breath of air, then turned her attention to Sara, who still sat on the floor on the other side of the pantry in a completely nonconfrontational manner.

"Don't look at me," Sara said. "I was brought up in Penwyck. I nursed tea at my mother's breast. My bladder can handle it just fine. He's the one who has to go."

Fawn hesitated, then rolled her eyes in a way that would make an American teenager proud. "Fine," she bit off in a likewise adolescent manner. "You can use the loo. Just don't try anything funny, as you've seen for yourself *you're* outnumbered and *we're* well armed."

"Yeah, with a thermos and basket of bread, no less," Shane said.

Without warning, she tossed both items in question at him. Shane caught them capably, and in turn, tossed them to Sara, who likewise snared them with ease. Then, his hands still extended straight out to his sides to show Fawn that he didn't plan to try anything funny—ha—he took a few slow steps toward the door...and her.

She backed up as he approached, then stepped aside to allow him through, never taking her eyes from his. Shane continued to move slowly, hands out to his sides, his gaze never shifting, until he was clear of the door. Then, in one swift, fluid motion, he grabbed Fawn and shoved her into the pantry, where Sara, without missing a beat, dispatched her with a thermos upside the head before she had a chance to make a sound. As she fell to the floor with a heavy thump, Sara tucked the thermos beneath one arm, then slipped the basket of bread over her other. Then she bent to tug off Fawn's flat shoes and slipped her own feet into them instead. Finally she brushed off her hands and stepped over the inert body, smiling as she neared Shane.

"My, but for some reason I enjoyed that quite a lot," she whispered when she stood beside him. "She has rather elephantine feet, but I should be able to keep her shoes on, I think." She dipped her chin toward Shane's feet then. He was still clad only in socks. "What about you?"

"I'll manage," he whispered back. "I have a tough hide. And I've spent most of my life running on hot sand and broken shells. I'll be okay." He tipped his head toward the back door on the other side of the kitchen. "Shall we go?"

"Yes, let's," Sara said, gripping both basket and thermos more firmly. "These people are frightfully bad hosts.

I think I can safely say that this is the worst party I've ever attended.''

Not surprisingly, when they reached the back door, they found that it was locked. So, without further ado, Shane kicked it—hard. The first kick did little more than alert anyone else who might be in the house that they were in the process of escaping. The second kick, however, blew the door off its lower hinge, and they immediately pushed through it and down the porch. It was twilight—and cold—but the sun hadn't set so far that they couldn't see what they were doing, or where they were going—even if they had no idea what they were doing or where they were going. Shane led the way, though, trusting Sara to follow. He figured they were equally matched here, neither of them knowing where they were or which way to go. So he headed through the backyard of the house, toward a heavily wooded area beyond.

They had just sprung through the trees when he heard an angry male voice—only one of them—coming from behind them. Instinctively, he reached behind himself and groped for Sara's hand, and twined his fingers fiercely with her own. Vaguely, as he tugged her through trees, over the rough terrain, he noticed not the pain that shot through his feet with every stray stick and stone, but how she seemed to have no trouble at all keeping up with him—even though he'd run cross-country track in both high school and college. Of course, the dense foliage hindered their progress, so speed wasn't so much an issue as dexterity. Nevertheless, Sara, he discovered, was both as speedy and as dexterous as he.

Neither said a word as they pummeled the wilderness and bore deeper into the woods, and he kept his ear tuned to their rhythmic, labored breathing to keep himself focused, instead of on the masculine voice that trailed them. Gradually, though, that voice began to ebb. Eventually, it disappeared completely. By then, night had well and truly fallen, and Shane knew it would soon be pointless to keep running. It was dark, it was cold and they had no idea where they were. So little by little, he slowed their pace until their steps became more deliberate.

His feet hurt like hell, which was another reason he needed to slow down. But his panic had lessened, and his instincts told him that they weren't in as precarious a situation as they had been upon fleeing the house. Certainly they weren't out of the woods yet—if one could pardon the incredibly stupid pun—but he didn't think it would be unwise for them to slow down and choose their route more carefully from here.

"How you doing?" he gasped in a rough whisper as he drew Sara up beside himself and came to a halt.

Reluctantly, he dropped her hand, settling both of his on his waist. He bent forward to assist his breathing for a moment, then straightened again. He could just barely make out her silhouette in the darkness and saw that she, too, was struggling to level off her breathing. She had placed both hands on a tree and was pushing against it, as if she were trying to work a few kinks out of her muscles. The basket of bread still swung from one arm, and the thermos, he could tell by her strangely altered profile, was shoved down the front of her blouse. He couldn't help smiling when he saw it. Awfully quick thinking on her part.

"I'm all right," she said, her voice as low and labored as his own. "Just winded. How are your feet?"

They hurt like hell, Shane thought again. "Fine," he told her. "But I wouldn't balk at a chance to get off them for a while. Any chance you've become psychic over the last couple of hours and know exactly where we are and how to get out of here?"

He wasn't sure, but he thought she chuckled at that. "Sorry. No. But if we could perhaps get a good look at the sky, I might be able to figure our bearings."

They both looked up, but a dense umbrella of crisscrossing tree branches hindered any sight they might have of the night sky.

"How about X-ray vision?" he asked. "Developed that anytime recently, by any chance?"

"Drat it, no," Sara told him. "All I have is this pesky gold rope that induces people to tell the truth. Wouldn't you know. Damn our luck."

"Ah, well," he said. "At least we still have our senses of humor."

"And our lives," she added.

"Also a very good thing to have," he agreed.

She took another few minutes to steady her breathing, then said, "I'm not certain, but I think we've been heading up a mountain."

"Felt that way to me, too," Shane said.

"And I can't help thinking, too," she continued, "that we should probably be heading *down* a mountain instead."

He nodded reluctantly. He'd known that, but he'd been more concerned with just getting them away from the house at the time instead of going in the right direction. "Yeah, I agree with you there, too. I'm wondering, though, if we wouldn't be better off waiting until morning. I think we lost our captors for now. But I also think they'll be after us again once the sun comes up. It would be better if we saw them first."

"Agreed," Sara said.

"So. Ever spent a night under the stars?" he asked.

Even in the darkness, he could see her shaking her head. "No. I always thought that if I chose to sleep under stars, it would be Tom Cruise or George Clooney."

Shane laughed out loud at that and made himself not say the thing he really wanted to say, which was that he might not be a star, but he sure wouldn't mind if she…

Instead he replied, "Yeah, well, trust me. This will be even better."

"I sincerely doubt it," she said.

"Aw, c'mon, where's that General Wallington spirit, huh?"

"I left it in the pantry. It got caught beneath the unconscious Fawn of the elephantine feet. I don't see it getting up anytime soon.''

"We'll be fine out here," Shane promised her, even though he was far from believing that himself. "I think I can even remember how they taught me to start a fire with two sticks when I was in Cub Scouts.''

"My, but you do know how to impress a girl on the first date," Sara said. "Fire from sticks? It boggles.''

"So does this mean you'll invite me up for a nightcap later?''

"First things first. I need to make sure you can do that stick thing you promised.''

They spent the next half hour or so creeping through the brush, listening to see if they were still being followed. They looked for a clearing that might offer them a view of the night sky, or some kind of shelter that might make their stay more comfortable—and safe—during the night. Finally they came to an area overhung by mossy rocks that lay facing the opposite direction from which they'd come.

By then, Shane hadn't heard a sound for a long time other than the ones they'd made themselves, and he was confident they'd lost their pursuers—at least until morning. He didn't think they'd be taking too big a risk if they started a small fire to ward off the worst of the cold and darkness that had descended, especially in the sanctuary of an overhang. They could eat their dinner of hard bread and weak tea, maybe get a little shut-eye, then set out again when the sun came up—hopefully in the *right* direction this time.

As he searched for a couple of likely fire sticks, Sara scraped brush and rocks away from a flat area beneath one of the wider-hanging stones. As he tried to remember enough of his early scouting experience to turn the fire sticks he finally found into a stick fire, she unpacked their meager dinner and arranged it on the ground in a way that would have made a five-star restaurant's maitre d' proud. And as they finished consuming that meager dinner, and the flames of the fire began to burn low, Shane realized he was fit to be tied. Literally. At least, his feet were. Preferably with antiseptic-soaked bandages.

Sara seemed to notice the condition of his feet right about the time that last thought formed in his brain. "Oh my God," she said, crawling around the fire to where Shane had propped his feet on a rock to catch some of its warmth. Gingerly, she lifted one foot in her hand, noting the blood-stained sock. "You told me your feet were all right."

"They were all right when you asked," he lied.

"They were not," she countered. "They've been bleeding. That obviously didn't start just now."

"Yeah, but they were numb when you asked me, so I didn't know they were hurt," he qualified.

"Liar," she replied succinctly. "You cut them to ribbons while we were running. Why didn't you say something?"

"Well, gee, I was kinda busy at the time," he pointed out. "There was somebody chasing me who probably would have killed me if he caught me, and that sorta took my attention away from other matters." He reined in his irritation—though whether that irritation was for Sara or himself, he couldn't quite say—and added, "Besides, what would we have done? Stop running? Go slower? Be more careful so I don't hurt my widdle footsies? I don't think so."

She made a face at him. "You wear Fawn's shoes tomorrow. As I said, her feet were on the elephantine side, so they might even fit you."

"I'll be okay," he said. "You keep Fawn's shoes." He grinned at her. "They don't match my belt at all."

"They took your belt," Sara pointed out, grinning back at him in spite of herself.

"All the more reason not to wear the shoes," he replied. "I'd be a walking, talking fashion-don't."

Sara didn't think Shane's comment really commanded a reply, so she said nothing as she gently stripped away the socks from both of his feet. Evidently, she wasn't gentle enough, however, as she heard him wince a few times as she worked. Once she had the socks removed, the scant light provided by the shrinking fire revealed just how badly he had been lying about their condition. They were a mess, crisscrossed with scrapes and cuts and streaked with dried blood.

There was still a spot of tea left in the thermos, so she reached for it and unscrewed the top. She started to remove her sweater, thinking she'd soak a corner of it with the tepid liquid and clean his feet. Then she realized she'd be better off hanging on to the warmer garment and using her blouse for bandages.

"Be right back," she said suddenly, standing.

Obviously confused by her action, Shane said, "Wait a minute. Where are you going?"

Sara thrust a thumb over her shoulder. "Behind the rock for a moment. I have something I need to do."

She left him to interpret that as he would, then retreated into the darkness to remove a few things—her stockings were a mess, too, after all—and then don her sweater again. She buttoned the cardigan up to its top button at the crew neck, and returned with her shirt in her hands.

"One hundred percent silk," she said as she ripped it in two. "*And* it's Ralph Lauren. It should make excellent bandages."

"But—"

She cut off whatever he had intended to add by ripping the shirt again, therefore making whatever objection he might utter a moot point. When she had a half-dozen strips of fabric for each foot, she balled up what was left of her blouse and used it as a washcloth. Very carefully, she bathed first one foot and then the other, doing her best to ignore Shane's hisses and muttered grunts of discomfort.

When she finished her ablutions, she used the strips of fabric she'd torn to carefully wrap each of his feet. Then she propped both of them back atop the smooth rock he had placed near the fire, as they had been before. But when she glanced up to see how he was faring, her breath caught suddenly in her throat. His face was half-cast in shadow, but even so, she could see that his eyes had grown darker and heavy-lidded. He was focused wholly on her face, and even through the faint light, she saw something in his expression that was both appealing and somehow menacing. Something that in fact seemed to be rather…arousing? And also perhaps…aroused?

Oh, dear…

"Ah…does that feel better?" she asked, her voice coming out as a bare squeak.

Shane nodded slowly in response. But he said nothing. He only continued to gaze at her in that arousing, aroused manner, something that had the effect on Sara of making her feel aroused, too.

Oh, dear…

She swallowed with some difficulty and tried to tell herself she was only imagining things. She was only imagining the slow heat that had begun to wind through her the moment she looked up to find him staring at her. She was only imagining the way that heat seemed to be lighting little fires in its wake, all throughout her body. She was only imagining the way she wished she could touch him as intimately elsewhere as she had his feet. She was only imagining how much she wished he would take her into his arms and hold her. Kiss her. And also—

"Is there…is there anything…anything else I can do for you?" she stammered, putting a halt to her errant thoughts before they wandered too far into dangerous territory. "To…to make you more…more comfortable, I mean?"

Again Shane nodded slowly in response to her nervous question. But still he said nothing to clarify his, ah, needs.

"And, um…what might that, uh, be?" she made herself ask.

For a moment, he still didn't reply, though he continued to gaze at her as if he were unable to look anywhere else.

And the longer he studied her, the more anxious and aroused Sara became. Good heavens, how could he make her feel so needy and wanton without even touching her? Without even saying a word? Other men had used far more sophisticated means in an attempt to seduce her, yet Shane Cordello didn't even have to crook his little finger to make her want to capitulate to him completely. How could that be?

When he remained silent, she began to wonder if maybe her voice had grown as weak as her body felt, and she hadn't even been able to project it the few feet necessary to reach his ears. She was about to utter the question again—if only she could remember now what it was she had asked him—when finally he spoke up.

But all he said was "Come here," in a low, gravelly voice unlike any she had heard from him since their initial encounter. In fact, if she had thought he sounded aroused before, now he sounded like a man who was utterly intent on…

Good heavens. He sounded like a man who was intent on making love to the likeliest woman this very moment. Not that she had heaps of experience in recognizing how men sounded when they were intent on making love to the likeliest woman this very moment, but she wasn't a trembling virgin. Just a regular virgin, that was all. But that didn't mean she hadn't been physical with a man. She just hadn't been quite *that* physical with one. Nevertheless, she *did* recognize the sound of a man who was put on when she heard one. And Shane definitely sounded put on. Or something.

But how could a man get put on by having a woman wash his bloody feet? That wasn't sexual by any stretch of the imagination. Not for a woman, anyway. But men? Well, she had seen them become randy over something as innocuous as the shape of a pudding dessert. Still, maybe she didn't know that much about men after all.

"Wh-what did you say?" she asked, just in case maybe she *had* heard him incorrectly.

"Come here," he repeated, more loudly this time. More insistently this time. More commandingly. More arousingly…

Oh, *dear.*

Normally, when issued a command by someone other than her professors, Sara desisted. In fact, she often even desisted when her professors issued commands. She didn't like it when people told her what to do, regardless of the situation. Which, now that she thought about it, might not be such a good trait for a person to have when she wanted to join the RII. But that was beside the point. The point was that when Shane Cordello murmured, "Come here," every cell inside her leaped to respond. In the affirmative. Eagerly. It was as if there was an invisible string attached to both of them, and in speaking as he had, he had just tugged his end of that string. Hard. Because before she even realized what she was doing, she was crawling from her place at his feet up past the rest of him, toward his face.

"What?" she asked as she knelt by his right shoulder. "What is it you need me to do?"

He hesitated only a moment, then, in that same throaty, cajoling whisper, he said, "I need for you to lean down here closer."

Sara swallowed hard at the way his eyes seemed to grow even darker as he spoke. "Wh-why?" she asked, the word coming out a little breathless. A little languid. A little needy.

Oh, dear.

"Ah…wh-why do you need for me to do that?" she asked again.

He held her gaze firmly with his as he told her, "Because, Sara, I very much need to kiss you."

Seven

He very much needed to kiss her.

Oh, oh, oh, oh, dear.

Certain she must have misheard, Sara gazed steadily down into Shane's face in an effort to see if maybe her hearing was going...or if her wits had been completely addled by her ordeal. But she could tell right away from his expression that he had said exactly what she thought he'd said. Even more important, he had *meant* it.

"You...you...you..." she began. But she couldn't quite manage to do anything more than repeat that one little word, because her brain seemed to have shut down completely, even as other parts of her body were vaulting to life.

"I need to kiss you, Sara," he said again, even more loudly, insistently, commandingly and arousingly than before. "I want to kiss you. Lean down here so that I can."

And somehow, even as she told herself it was a bad idea, Sara did exactly as he asked...insisted...commanded...

whatever. Slowly, she bent forward, but she kept her palms flat on the ground, as if that might hold her anchored there—in reality, at safety. But as her face drew nearer to his, Shane reached up and curled his hand lightly over the nape of her neck, encouraging her closer still when she might have hesitated.

Ha, she thought as her mouth hovered over his. As if she would hesitate with something like this....

And then her mouth was on his, or perhaps his mouth was on hers, but really what difference did it make when such a wondrous sensation dashed through her body as a result? Had she felt cold before? she wondered vaguely. How odd. Because suddenly the most languorous warmth was winding throughout her body, from her mouth to her chest to her belly...and then to points beyond.

Shane kissed Sara in a way that she had never been kissed before, at once tentatively and tenaciously, both curiously and confidently. At first he seemed only to want a brief taste of her, because he only brushed his lips lightly across hers, once, twice, three times, before pulling slightly back again. When he broke contact, she opened her eyes, only to find him gazing enigmatically into her own. She felt herself smile, and then, instead of waiting for him to return to her, she dipped her head forward again and pressed her mouth to his.

The sensation that followed was quite exquisite.

The hand on her nape curled tighter, the fingers delving into her hair to weave through the errant strands and push her closer still. The rasp of his beard abraded her mouth, but his lips were soft...so soft and warm and inviting. Unable to help herself, Sara moved her hands from the ground and flattened her palms against his chest, marveling at the supple, solid musculature she felt beneath her fingertips. She had noticed right off how well built he was, thanks, presumably, to his line of work. And a number of times during the flight—and even after—she had felt her gaze wander toward him, to his bare arms and the flagrant biceps straining against the sleeves of his T-shirt. The snug garment had let her know, too, how impressively the rest of him was fashioned. And she had wondered—too often— how it would feel to be the woman lying beside, even beneath, such a man.

Here was her chance, she thought.

And then, without even realizing she had done it, she found herself stretched out alongside him, her entire body fitted to his. Shane reacted instantly, roping his other arm around her waist and pulling her half atop himself, splaying his hand open at the small of her back, as if he feared she would move away and wanted to anchor her in place.

Oh, no worries there, she wanted to tell him. She wasn't going anywhere. Not just yet…

She moved a hand to his hair and pushed her fingers through it, loving the feel of the silky tresses as they sifted over her flesh. Shane tilted his head and slanted his mouth over hers more possessively, intensifying the kiss as he pressed his mouth more intimately against hers. Again and again he kissed her, each kiss growing gradually more desperate than the one before, until his hunger for her seemed voracious. When Sara opened her mouth to gasp for breath, he thrust his tongue inside, tasting her tentatively at first, then with more passion. She was initially surprised by the invasion, and almost drew away. But there was something wholly erotic about the feel of him inside her that way, and she found herself opening to him more willingly, even venturing her own tongue inside his mouth, to enjoy a taste or two of him herself.

He groaned at her first penetration, moving the hand on her nape up to the crown of her head, to hold her in place for his own exploration. For long moments they warred for possession of the kiss, their tongues tangling and tantalizing, tasting and teasing. And then Sara felt herself spinning, landing on her back, and Shane crawling half atop her. The weight of him, bearing down on her breasts and pelvis and thighs, sent a zing of sensation pounding through her entire body—never had she felt so utterly aroused. As she looped her arms around his waist, he insinuated one of his legs between hers and dropped a hand to her hip. He propped himself up on one elbow, his forearm cradling her neck and urging her head back up to his.

And then he was well and truly in charge of the kiss, penetrating her mouth deeply again and again and again. The hand at her hip skimmed down to her thigh and lifted her leg over his. Sara enthusiastically complied, hooking the back of her knee over his in an effort to bring him closer still. When she did, Shane thrust his own leg higher, harder, against that most intimate part of her, creating a delicious friction unlike anything she'd ever felt before. This time it was Sara who groaned in response, first to the frenetic shot of heat that exploded between her legs, and then to the way it moved outward, shuddering throughout her body.

And then she felt his hand creeping higher again, over her waist, to the hem of her sweater. Without warning, he freed the bottom button, then the one above it, and the one above that. When he had exposed her bare abdomen, he flattened a warm hand against it, skimming his open palm over her sensitive flesh from one side to another. Heat followed wherever he touched her, combining with that below her waist to generate an almost atomic reaction inside her. And still he kissed her, harder, deeper, faster, and all Sara could do was cling to him and hope he never stopped.

Then more buttons were being freed on her sweater, until the garment gaped wide over her bra. Shane tore his mouth from hers and, gasping, dragged damp, openmouthed kisses over her jaw, her throat, her neck. And then he was kissing the plump flesh above her bra, curving his hand over the lacy fabric beneath to make it plumper still. Sara tangled her fingers in his hair, feeling nearly insensate at the sensations firing through her. His thigh pressed against her again, generating another frantic combustion between her legs.

By now her skirt had ridden up well over her hips, to nearly her waist, and along with her gaping sweater, made her feel exposed and vulnerable. And somewhere at the back of her fevered brain, Sara slowly began to realize what was happening. What would happen if she allowed Shane's exploration, and her own, to continue. And she knew she wasn't ready for it to happen. Not yet.

"No!" she cried as she pulled herself away from him. She pressed both hands against his chest and pushed hard, then scrambled up from beneath him, moving quickly to the other side of the now nearly dead fire. She pulled her sweater around her and tried to quell her breathing, slowly tempering the rapid, ragged gasps. But her thoughts spun so riotously through her head that they lacked coherence and meaning. She honestly didn't know what to say.

"We can't," she finally managed breathlessly. Because that realization, if no other, did become crystal clear. "We can't do this, Shane. We can't."

"Why not?" he demanded, his own breathing every bit as rasping and uneven as her own.

She groped for the first thing that might make sense. "The Black Knights," she said. "They could be any-where." Though she was confident they'd lost their pur-suers some time ago. "We must keep our wits about us," she added nonetheless—because that, at least, was true.

Oh, well-done, Sara, she then congratulated herself when she finally got the words out. *Blame it on the Black Knights. Good girl. Don't let him know it's your own sorry, fearful self you're really letting stand in the way.*

For a moment, she heard nothing from the other side of the fire except Shane's continued panting for breath. Then, very softly, "Right," he said. "Right. I don't guess it would be a good idea to let them catch us with our pants down."

She closed her eyes and wished very, very hard that he hadn't used that particular euphemism.

Evidently, he was rethinking it himself, because he quickly tried to backpedal. "I mean, uh…" he said.

But they both knew it was too late for that. Had their embrace gone much longer or much further, they would have been caught without considerably more than their pants. They would have been caught without their inhibitions, without their cares, without their good judgment. And the loss of those, Sara knew, would be infinitely worse than the loss of clothing.

"No harm done," she said, knowing full well what a horrendous lie that was. "Tensions are running high for both of us. It was bound to happen eventually."

Again, silence met her remarks for a moment, then, "Yeah, right," Shane said sarcastically. "Bound to happen. Tensions high. Nothing more than that."

"Right," she agreed dismally. "Nothing more than that."

She tried to button up her sweater, but it took longer than usual because her hands were trembling so ferociously. When she finally did turn to face Shane again, the fire was well and truly out—all of the fires, in fact, she couldn't help thinking—so that all she could decipher of him was a scant profile in the darkness that told her nothing of what he might actually be feeling.

Disappointment, no doubt, she thought, which, along with a host of other things, was what she was feeling herself. She just wished she knew if they felt disappointed about the same things. For Shane, as it would be for any man, it was probably his missing out on the physical coupling to which their embrace was a prelude that frustrated him most. He probably didn't care that it was Sara, specifically, with whom he'd be denied his coupling, only that his body told him to go for the most convenient available warm body, and suddenly that body wasn't there.

For Sara, though, disappointment took many forms. Yes, she, too, was frustrated to miss out on that physical coupling, but not just because it was what her body commanded her to do with the most readily accessible vessel. No, it was specifically Shane she wanted for that union, and no one else. She only wished she could tell if he felt the same way about her.

Not that she suspected for a moment that he was, like she, a virgin. But she would have liked to think that in making love to her, he would experience the same sort of "firstness" that she experienced herself. She wanted him to think making love with her was different from other women. She wanted him to think *she* was different from other women. She wanted him to think she was special to him. The way he was special to her.

Unfortunately, Sara just couldn't convince herself that that was true. The two of them were just so very different. And they each had obligations that might very well be insurmountable. Sara had looked forward to a career with the RII since she was a child on her father's knee, and that meant making a commitment unlike any she'd ever made before. Shane might very well be the new monarch of Penwyck, something that would require a massive commitment from him—if he accepted the position, and if indeed it was his to accept. They both had much to lose and much to sacrifice if they became involved. And Sara, for one, knew she had to give great thought to what lay ahead before she could surrender herself so completely—to Shane or any man.

Though, at the moment, she doubted there would ever be any man but Shane to whom she wanted to surrender.

She lifted a hand to rub her weary eyes. Sleep. She needed sleep. They both did. Neither could trust anything that happened when they were exhausted and running on adrenaline. It was no wonder they'd turned to each other the way they had. It *could* have happened to anyone. Really, it could. Truly.

"We should probably sleep in shifts," Shane said, as if he'd read her mind. "I'm a little, ah…wired myself, so why don't you go first?"

"All right," Sara said reluctantly. Not that she thought she was any more inclined to sleep herself. Still, she did feel so very tired. Maybe if she just closed her eyes for a bit...

She lay down where she stood—well away from Shane Cordello. She knew that with the night being so cool, it would make more sense for the two of them to lay side by side and collect each other's body heat. But considering what other kind heat would no doubt be generated by such a position, she'd probably be better off sleeping over here, in the cold. So she made herself as comfortable as she could, folding one arm beneath her head to use as a pillow, clutching her sweater tightly around her.

Tomorrow, she thought, things would make more sense. Tomorrow, in the light of day, all would be much clearer. Tomorrow, they could find their way down the mountain and hopefully to some sort of village or settlement. And then...

She sighed heavily as her eyelids drooped. Well, she'd think about *and then* tomorrow.

Evidently by silent and mutual consent when they set off the following morning, neither Sara nor Shane spoke a word about what had happened. There were times when Shane thought he had dreamed the embrace they'd shared the night before, so elusive and unreal did it seem. And then there were other times when he knew it had happened—he could relive every touch and taste of Sara—but was forced to acknowledge that it had been a mistake. Only problem was, he couldn't quite make himself believe it had been a mistake. Because how could something that felt so good, so right, so perfect, have ever been a mistake? In either event, he was relieved Sara seemed as unwilling to discuss it as he was himself. Because regardless of the circumstances, it shouldn't have happened.

Not yet, anyway.

Still, it was better for the two of them to focus for now

on the immediate future and not on any part of the past. They had no idea where they were, and there was every reason to believe that the kidnappers were still looking for them. The Black Knights, too, probably knew the area fairly well—certainly better than Shane and Sara did—so they'd know where to look for the escapees. If nothing else, they were smart enough to figure out that Shane and Sara would be headed *down* the mountain by now, and they'd be on the lookout for them. Shane and Sara had no choice but to simply forge ahead, keep their eyes and ears open and hope like hell that their luck lasted.

The day was long and tedious, with little conversation between the two of them. Shane didn't know if that was because they both felt awkward following last night's embrace, or if they were both just anxious about staying one step ahead of the Black Knights or if they were both simply concentrating on the terrain and the direction of the sun. Probably a combination of all three, he thought. Again, though, he was grateful for the preoccupation. Because his main focus right now had to be on finding their way home, and not on how good it had felt to hold Sara the night before, how sweet she had tasted, how warm and soft her flesh had been, how very much he wanted to—

Damn. *Focus, Cordello,* he told himself. *Focus.*

It was growing dark—and cold—again by the time they wandered out of the woods and into a clearing…that emptied into the yard of a farmhouse in the distance. A farmhouse whose chimney ousted a steady plume of smoke, and in whose windows burned a pale yellow light. By Shane's and Sara's reactions, one might have thought they had just stumbled onto the open—and unguarded—gold vault at Fort Knox. Although still a good mile distant from the house, they each exclaimed their delight upon seeing it before hastening their step to reach it—even Shane, because the realization that they might finally be rescued from this damned predicament somehow dulled the pain in his feet.

As they drew nearer to the house, he saw that although

it was a good-size, two-story structure, it was by no means elaborate: a white stucco construction with an honest-to-goodness thatched roof, dusty walkway and stone fence encompassing the perimeter of its small, grassy yard. Vines grew thickly over part of the front and on one side of the house, and bushes brimming with fat red berries grew rampant beneath window boxes bursting with chrysanthemums in gold and scarlet and yellow. Had Sara not assured him already that they were on the Continent, Shane would have sworn they'd somehow found themselves in Scotland, so quaintly British did the scene first appear.

The house's style upon further inspection, however, didn't look especially British. It was a plain square box, with plain square windows that were shuttered on the western side where the setting sun would have shone directly in. Still, as far as he was concerned, finding this secluded, deserted little place was better than finding the Playboy mansion at full party power. He'd never been so happy to see the appearance of a building in his life—not even one he was putting up himself. As they approached the front gate, however, Sara's pace slowed, until she finally came to a halt before even opening it.

"What's wrong?" Shane asked when she placed her hand gently over his upper arm to stop him. He halted with his hand affectionately stroking the old iron gate handle, but he nodded toward the house and said, "The end is in sight. Why are we stopping?"

"We have to be careful," she said.

He gaped at her. "Are you serious? What, do you think the Black Knights feverishly built and aged an old farmhouse overnight just to lure us inside and catch us that way?"

"No," she replied tersely, "but it's best to be cautious. If nothing else, people who live in secluded areas like this can be suspicious of strangers. Especially strangers who look like us."

Shane had no choice but to agree. Her sweater and skirt

were torn and soiled, her face, legs and hands were scratched and dirty, her hair hung in straggles around her shoulders. And hell, she was the better kept of the two of them. He was shoeless, his feet were a mess, and his blue jeans, T-shirt and jacket were more crumpled and ripped up than her clothing was. He could only imagine what his face looked like, but his cheeks were itchy with the overgrowth of his beard. He hadn't shaved for days. Hadn't bathed, either, he recalled, and neither had Sara, so they were both probably a little underwhelming as prospects for house guests.

"We have to have some excuse to explain our appearance," she said, evidently reading his mind. "Even if it's a nice family, they're going to wonder who's shown up at their door looking like this, and why."

"We can tell them we were camping," he said off the top of his head. "We were hiking through Europe. We're probably a little too old to pass ourselves off as college students—even if that's what you are—but maybe we could say we're honeymooners or something."

"Hiking honeymooners?" Sara asked skeptically.

He shrugged. "Sure. Happens all the time in my country."

"Mmm."

"So, anyway, we're hiking honeymooners," he continued unperturbed, "and then, suddenly, we're set upon. By, uh…by bears. Yeah, that's it."

Sara smiled. "I don't think they have bears here."

"Oh."

"And why would I be hiking in a skirt?" she added. "Not to mention that neither of us has appropriate footwear. You don't even have *in*appropriate footwear."

Okay, so she had a point. "Then what do you suggest?"

"I think the honeymoon part is fine," she said thoughtfully. "But we need something other than bears setting upon us. Something like…" Her eyes widened jubilantly. "Something like thieves perhaps," she said. "Modern-day highwaymen. They're certainly credible, if not common, in this part of the world. We were *driving* through the mountains—'' she began their story again ''—enjoying the views, when we were forced off the road by someone who followed us. We're honeymooning after all,'' she pointed out, ''so we wouldn't be paying attention to whether or not we were being followed, would we? We'd have our minds on other things.''

As if by mutual consent, their gazes flew to each other and locked, and Shane knew they both certainly did have their minds on other things at that moment. One other thing in particular, in fact. The kiss they had shared the night before.

Kiss nothing, he thought further. That had been a full-fledged body exploration, a grope of monumental proportions. It had also been very enlightening. Still, he couldn't imagine what had come over him to have let it happen in the first place, let alone go on as long as it had. Not that Sara hadn't seemed to enjoy it, too—until she put a stop to it. But they'd both completely forgotten the seriousness and precariousness of their situation, and that could have cost them both their lives.

Shane just hadn't been able to help himself, though. At the time it happened, he hadn't cared, quite frankly, where they were or how dire their circumstances happened to be. All he'd cared about in that moment was Sara. As he'd watched her bathing and bandaging his feet, as he'd observed her elegant, manicured hands working over his broken and bloodied flesh, as he'd felt her heat mingling with his own, as he'd noted their differences and seen how easily and perfectly those differences seemed to meld together... As he'd taken all of that in, the only thing he'd wanted was to have her hands—and her heat—on other parts of his body, mingling and melding with them, too. And then, when the pressure of her fingers on his feet had increased, had grown more intimate, more attentive, he hadn't been able to keep himself from thinking about touching her, too.

Suddenly nothing had mattered except touching Sara. Kissing Sara. Holding Sara.

Having Sara.

But he hadn't had her. Not that he wouldn't have taken her right there in the dirt last night, mindless of anything else, if she hadn't pulled away when she had. He was glad now, though, that she, at least, had been strong enough to put a halt to things before they went too far. Because now Shane was of the opinion that the first time the two of them made love, shouldn't be in the dirt, shouldn't be while they were on the run, shouldn't be while they were worrying over whether or not they'd make it through the night alive. No, when Shane finally made love to Sara—and he *would* make love to Sara, he promised himself—it was going to be in a soft bed where they were safe and comfortable, where they could focus entirely on each other, and take their time doing all the things they wanted to do.

"So we, ah...we were set upon by highwaymen," she hastily continued, pulling him abruptly out of what had promised to be a very nice—if untimely—little fantasy, "and they stole our car and all of our belongings. Then they left us stranded in the mountains, and we had to find our own way back down, and that's how we ended up at their front door. What do you think?"

Shane mulled her story over for a moment, then nodded. "Sounds as likely as anything else we might come up with. You sure you speak the language?"

"No worries there," she assured him.

"Then what are we waiting for?"

Sara inhaled what looked like a deep, fortifying breath, then smiled a tremulous little smile he supposed was meant to look encouraging. Then she took his hand in hers—reminding him that they were honeymooners, after all, as if she didn't want him to misinterpret the gesture—and they began to make their way toward the house. When they stood at the front door, she used her free hand to smooth over her clothing and hair as best she could—which, Shane noticed, wasn't all that successful a gesture—then lifted a hand to knock.

After a moment, the door creaked inward, and a stout, silver-haired woman greeted them. She wore a straight black skirt and white blouse, heavy black shoes and a brightly embroidered shawl hung around her shoulders. Her hair was pulled straight back from her face in a bun that sat high atop the back of her head, and she was smiling a curious, but warm, smile.

"¿Sí?" she said.

"Buenos tardes, señora," Sara began.

About that time, a stout, silver-haired man joined the woman, his attire similar to her own—black pants, white shirt, black shoes. But instead of a shawl, he wore a battered brown vest. His smile was also inquiring but courteous, so Sara smiled in turn and included him in her greeting, as well.

What followed was a rapid barrage of Spanish that was much too fast for Shane to follow, even though he spoke the language well enough to make occasional forays into Tijuana. He caught a word here and there, though, enough to assure him that Sara was telling the couple the story about the thieves and their being left stranded. She must have been convincing—hey, even Shane thought she looked earnest and distressed—because the elderly couple's expressions went from wary to shocked to pitying. Finally, the woman clucked a few times over Sara and cupped a hand on her shoulder, reached over to give Shane a maternal pat on the cheek and showed them both inside.

The interior of the house was as simple and modest as the outside, but it was utterly inviting nonetheless. The floors were fashioned of terra-cotta tiles, the furniture was boxy and old and functional. But there were warm touches and splashes of color present in painted clay pots full of plants and flowers, the wrought-iron candlesticks and sconces, photographs of—Shane presumed—children and grandchildren, and brightly woven wool rugs. The walls were whitewashed and unadorned, but the vista of sunset-splashed trees and mountains viewed through the open windows was warm and beautiful and really commanded no further decoration for the room.

The conversation between the other three continued as Shane absorbed all of this, so he just did his best to keep smiling and being as nonthreatening as he could when he remembered how he must look and smell. After some minutes, the elderly man nodded in response to something his wife said, then headed up a flight of steps on the other side of the room. The woman took Sara's hand and led her over to a rocking chair near the fireplace, saying something over her shoulder to Shane that he figured meant he should follow. She sat Sara down in the chair, said a few more words, then strode off toward a door that led, judging by the delicious smells coming through it, to the kitchen.

"Hilda is bringing us something to eat," Sara said. "Enrique is her husband. Their last name is Santos. I told them what happened—I mean, what we agreed to say happened—and they've insisted we stay the night, since it's nearly dark. She said the closest town is an hour's walk, and Enrique can't drive at night. Hilda can't drive at all. So really, it would be foolish for us to try and go any farther tonight if we can avoid it. But they don't have a telephone, unfortunately, so we have no way to contact anyone." Her expression grew even more concerned as she added, "I hate putting them out this way, Shane. They obviously have very little, yet they've generously offered to share with us what they can. I feel terrible lying to them like this."

"You think they'd feel better if you told them there are kidnappers and hijackers in them thar hills?" he asked.

"Well, no…"

"Look, if it makes you feel better, Sara, you can tell them the truth tomorrow, before we leave. And you can send them a check or a fruit basket or something when we get to Penwyck to pay them back for their hospitality."

She sighed heavily and lifted a hand to her head, apparently trying to rub away a headache. Then she pushed her fingers back through her hair and grimaced.

"Ugh," she said. "I'm filthy dirty. We should both wash up before we eat anything." She glanced down at her attire. "I just wish we had some other clothes to put back on once we've cleaned up. Rather defeats the purpose, doesn't it?"

Having evidently anticipated the problem—and, of course, how could he not have, seeing the way Shane and Sara looked and smelled—Enrique came back downstairs then, with several articles of clothing strewn over both arms. He grinned as he approached Sara and extended the ones on his right arm toward her, then leveled the others toward Shane, who smiled his thanks with a softly uttered *"Gracias."* Sara did likewise. Then she and Enrique enjoyed another brief exchange in Spanish before she turned back to Shane.

"The clothes belonged to their children, who've grown and moved away. Enrique said we can wash up in a bathroom upstairs, and that they have a spare room for us up there, as well. I told him we'd rather clean up before we eat, so do you want to have a go?"

Shane shook his head. "Nah. Ladies first."

And never in his life had the phrase held more truth than it did in that moment. Because even filthy and ah, malodorous, her hair tangled and her clothing torn, Sara Wallington was the classiest lady he'd ever met in his life, and she was definitely first and foremost in his thoughts—and had been since he'd first laid eyes on her. When she stood up from the chair, it was with the imperiousness of a monarch, and when she offered another quiet *"Gracias"* to Enrique, she did it with such dignity and nobility that she might very well have been Queen of Penwyck herself.

Man. What a woman.

No sooner had the thought formed in Shane's head when Enrique spoke it aloud in his native language. Shane chuckled and, in what he hoped was correct Spanish, managed to agree. The two shared a stilted dialogue about the area, the weather and how dastardly highwaymen could be, but when the conversation turned to how enjoyable the newlywed state was, and what a lucky man Shane was to have landed such a wonderful girl, he forced himself to change the subject. Not that he didn't agree that Sara was a wonderful girl—*au contraire*. And he didn't doubt for a moment that the newlywed state could be exceptionally enjoyable—for those who were that way inclined. And he was indeed certainly a lucky man—for a variety of reasons.

So it wasn't the actual subject matter of Enrique's conversational side trip that Shane objected to. It just made him uneasy to group all of those thoughts together into one conversational side trip, especially one that included Sara. He knew it was necessary for them to lie. If they'd told the truth, the Santoses probably wouldn't have believed them. Or, worse, the Santoses *would* have believed them and been terrified for their own lives. And Shane truly didn't think the elderly couple was at risk—if he thought that, he wouldn't be here endangering them, and he and Sara would have suffered another night on the road.

So it wasn't the lie itself that troubled Shane. In fact, it hadn't bothered him a bit to perpetrate the fabrication before he'd entered the house. Now, however, for some reason, the lie was making him feel wholly uncomfortable. And perpetrating it on Hilda and Enrique suddenly didn't seem right.

Fortunately, Sara returned surprisingly quickly from her shower, dressed in the clothes the Santoses had provided, courtesy of their daughter. Now a full, flowered skirt in a dozen shades of green and blue danced around her calves, and a loose-fitting shirt the same pale green as her eyes scooped low over her breasts. Her hair was still damp, but she had smoothed it back from her face and braided it, the long plaited tresses falling over one shoulder and nearly to the neckline of her shirt. A few errant wisps curled around her face, and coupled with the more feminine clothing than the tailored look she'd worn before—pink sweater notwithstanding—she seemed to have a softer, more ethereal appearance. Seeing her like this now, she looked so much younger, so much sweeter, so much more ingenuous, so...so...so...

Wow. That was the best word Shane could think of in that moment to describe what she was. She just looked really, really *wow.*

''Bath's all yours,'' she said. But although the remark was clearly intended for Shane—it was spoken in English, after all—her gaze ricocheted wildly around the room, as if she were looking at everything *except* him. As if she felt too nervous to meet his gaze. As if she were uncomfortable for some reason. But how could that be? he wondered. Right now, she should be feeling better than she had in days. Somehow, though, she seemed more anxious than ever.

Shane turned to Enrique to thank him again for his hospitality, then back to Sara. But she still wasn't looking at him, still seemed to be very apprehensive about something. She toyed with the end of her braid and shifted her weight from one foot to the other then back again. So he only smiled and said, ''Thanks, I won't be long,'' and headed for the stairs. And when he passed by Sara, he tried not to notice how good she smelled, all womanly and fresh and warm. And he tried hard not to think about how the Santoses had promised them a room for the night—singular. And he tried very hard not to worry about how it was probably going to be a long, long time until morning.

Eight

Oh, dear. Oh, dear, oh, dear, oh, dear.

Sara couldn't believe how nervous she was, just because she was in the same room with Shane—a kitchen, no less, probably the most harmless room in a house when it came to social hazards. And it wasn't like they were even having any potentially hazardous social interaction, either. No, he was simply seated across the table from her, sipping his gazpacho with utter calm, as if he hadn't a care in the world. Yet that seemed to be the very thing that was making her feel so anxious and uneasy. Here she'd been through all manner of uncomfortable, even dangerous, experiences in the last few days, but never had she felt more apprehensive than she did now, seated at a dinner table across from a handsome man, watching him eat.

And, truth be told, she could pinpoint the exact second when that apprehension had begun: the moment she'd stepped out of the bathtub and realized that her underwear was much too rank to put back on, so she'd have to do without it completely.

Oh, dear. Oh, dear, oh, dear, oh, dear.

Enrique, apparently, hadn't thought about undergarments when he'd gone in search of clothing for her and Shane to wear. And Sara, for some reason, was hesitant to ask Hilda about it. She didn't know if it was because of some misplaced modesty, or if it was because the question might seem odd coming from a newlywed, or if it was because she felt as if they'd asked the couple for too much already. Maybe it was because of something else entirely that she was better off not thinking about. In any event, it left her sitting here looking at Shane and wearing no underwear, and somehow, the combination just made her feel—

Well…best not to think about that, either.

And then, to make matters even more difficult, as Sara had exited the bathroom, she'd bumped into Hilda coming down the hall, and her hostess had told her she'd just made up a room for the honeymooners. *Un dormitorio,* she had said. A bedroom, Sara had translated. *One* bedroom. *Por los recién casados.* For the newlyweds. For her and Shane. To share.

What it had amounted to was two people, one room, zero underwear. And that added up to trouble.

Oh, dear. Oh, dear, oh, dear, oh, dear.

She really should have thought a little further ahead when she and Shane had concocted their story, she thought now. But it had sounded so likely and credible the first time. It still did. A good number of honeymooners came to Europe to drive through the mountains. And being set upon by thieves wasn't *too* awfully wild a scenario. The problem was that honeymooners, Sara was reasonably certain, stayed together in the same room when they traveled, regardless of what country they happened to be visiting, especially in Europe, where—one could very realistically argue—romance had been born. Ergo…

Ergo, she should have realized upon conceiving the story

that she and Shane would be spending the night together in the same room. The same bed. And she, at least, wouldn't be wearing any underwear. Nor, it was probably safe to conclude, would he. Of course, it probably wasn't realistic to think she might have anticipated that last bit, regardless of how farsighted she might have been in dreaming up the rest. And had they actually *been* honeymooners, the lack of underwear wouldn't really have been a problem. But she and Shane weren't honeymooners.

Not yet, anyway.

Not *ever!* she immediately corrected herself. There was no way she would be performing any deeds with him—tonight or any other night—that might be misconstrued as honeymoon behavior by anyone. Well, except maybe holding hands and smiling in a simpering fashion, just to make it look convincing to the Santoses. But once the two of them were behind closed doors, with one bed and zero underwear…

Oh, dear. Oh, dear, oh, dear, oh, dear.

Oh, why hadn't she made it clear to Hilda that they would need separate rooms? Sara asked herself as she lifted a spoonful of the spicy cold soup to her own mouth and tried *very* hard not to look at Shane and think about how she wasn't wearing any underwear and, probably, neither was he. Why couldn't she have come up with the idea that they were bickering honeymooners? That they'd been arguing when the thieves set upon them, and now they were picking up where they'd left off and weren't speaking to each other? All right, she supposed perhaps that might have been stretching it a bit. Still, she should have realized how badly she was about to step in it before she let her foot hit the ground.

Goodness. Hindsight really was twenty-twenty.

And now she would be spending the night in a room with a man whom she found much too attractive, and she wouldn't have any underwear to keep her warm. Not that warmth was really her primary concern with regards to the undergarment. Maybe Shane would do his best to help keep her warm....

Stop it, she commanded herself. *You're behaving like a schoolgirl.*

Of course, maybe that was because Shane Cordello made her *feel* like a schoolgirl. One just bursting with hormonal pubescent awareness of everything that happens between a boy and a girl, especially when they're stranded in a room together with no under—

Stop it, Sara!

The mental declaration was so loud as it reverberated through her brain that Sara actually lost her grip on her spoon, and it went tumbling to the floor. Hilda began to rise, to pick it up, but Sara stopped her and scooped up the utensil herself, replacing it on the table with trembling hands. By then she'd nearly finished the entire bowl of gazpacho—her second—anyway, and a big chunk of hard brown bread besides. On top of her nervous queasies, she really had had more than enough to satisfy her. Enough food, anyway. She wasn't hungry anymore. Not in the traditional sense, at least.

Oh, she really did have to get a grip.

"Finished?" Shane asked from the opposite side of the table.

She flinched at the question in spite of herself, then nodded in response. But she didn't look at him. She didn't have to. The image of him was imprinted staunchly at the forefront of her brain. Most specifically, the image of him returning from his own bath earlier was imprinted staunchly at the forefront of her brain. He'd come downstairs still completing the act of donning his shirt over loose-fitting khaki trousers that hung low on his hips—evidently Julio Santos, the Santoses' son, was a bit broader at the waist than Shane was. The shirt, too, fashioned of brown and gold madras plaid, was loose fitting, something she'd noted as he'd buttoned it up while approaching her.

Before she'd forced herself to look away, though, Sara

had been privy to a generous glimpse of dark hair coiling across his chest and abdomen, disappearing into the low-riding waistband of his trousers, along with a set of perfectly delineated abdominals that had left her mouth dry. He'd swept his still-damp, dark hair straight back from his face, but one wayward curl had fallen over his forehead. He had shaven, revealing a long slashing dimple on each side of his mouth when he smiled, traits she hadn't noticed until then, traits that made him seem even sexier somehow. His eyes had looked even bluer, too, though she was certain she must have only imagined that. All in all, he offered a very appealing package. One she'd found herself wanting very badly to open.

Especially since she assumed there was no underwear beneath it.

Oh, do stop, Sara. You're embarrassing yourself.

She heard him moving on the other side of the table and braved a glimpse at him from the corner of her eye. Immediately she regretted the action, as he had launched himself into a full-body stretch that thrust his well-hewn chest forward and his arms to his sides, arms that were corded with muscle and sinew. Arms Sara couldn't help recalling had felt so wonderfully tender when he'd held her the night before.

"Well, I don't know about you," he said as he relaxed and pushed his chair away from the table. He turned his attention directly to Sara, and she was helpless not to meet his gaze. Then, very softly, very meaningfully, he added, "But I think I'm ready for bed."

Oh, dear. Oh, dear, oh, dear, oh, dear.

"Ah, yes. Yes. Sleep would indeed be very welcome," she agreed. Then, *Liar,* she immediately berated herself. Sleep was the last thing she had in mind at the moment. She just hoped Shane's intended use for a bed didn't echo the one her own feverish brain kept replaying.

She explained to her hosts that they wanted to turn in, and Hilda and Enrique—with knowing little smiles that *re-*

ally made Sara nervous now—nodded and said their good-nights. Hilda added that their own room was downstairs, toward the back of the house, so if she and Shane needed anything—wink, wink, nudge, nudge—they'd have to come downstairs to find them. That, of course, only made Sara even *more* anxious, as she realized now how very secluded she and Shane would be upstairs. In the bedroom. With one bed. And no underwear.

Oh, dear…

She stood with so much speed and clumsiness that her chair went careening backward and crashed to the floor. The Santoses both started at the action, but Shane only smiled. Smiled knowingly, too, Sara couldn't help noticing. Then she realized she *was* noticing, which meant she was looking at him, which meant that her mouth went dry, her brain went numb and the rest of her went hot all over.

Had she thought herself nervous before? Goodness, that was nothing compared to what she felt now.

Because now Shane was gazing at her in a way he hadn't ever gazed at her before, with an intimacy and erudition that weakened every muscle she possessed. Her heart began to race, speeding blood through her body at an alarming rate, and she found herself feeling a little light-headed. She felt almost as if she were walking through a dream when she moved to right her chair and circle the table to where he stood waiting for her. He held out his hand at her approach, and automatically she took it. Then, after each of them uttered a soft *"Buenos noches"* to their hosts, they left the kitchen, moved silently through the living room, up the stairs and down the hallway, and finally into their bedroom.

With one bed.

"I can sleep on the floor," Shane said as he closed the door behind them, when he must have realized what she was thinking. "God knows it won't be any worse than sleeping in the dirt last night. At least we'll be warm here. And safe."

Sara turned to face him...and immediately wished she hadn't. The only light in the room came from the pale yellow halo of a small lamp near the bed, and it washed Shane in such a hazy glow that he seemed almost unreal somehow. Certainly more approachable than he had seemed before. Softer, gentler, more tender, less intimidating. Shaven, he didn't appear quite as dangerous as he previously had, but in some ways that made him more dangerous still, as Sara wanted more than anything to draw nearer and lift a hand to touch that fine skin. In place of the rebel's jeans and T-shirt, he wore the clothes of a student, and that, too, seemed to make him less threatening. He was leaning back against the door as if he were trying to keep out all the world's frights. And his smile... Oh, his smile. His smile held the promise of unearthly delights. She only wished she knew if he were capable of making other promises, as well. And more importantly, was he capable of keeping them?

"No," Sara said, surprising herself. "You don't have to sleep on the floor, Shane. Especially since you did sleep in the dirt last night. It's a big enough bed for both of us."

Barely, she added to herself. It didn't even appear to be a traditional double-size mattress. It was, however, larger than a single. Sort of.

His smile broadened, and something in her chest constricted tight. "Especially if we squinch up real close," he said.

And, oh, how she wished he hadn't. Mainly because it was exactly the same thing she was thinking herself. "Shane..." she began. But she really wasn't sure what she wanted to tell him. There were too many thoughts tumbling through her head for her to latch on to any one of them and try to understand what they meant.

Which really didn't seem to matter to Shane, as he cut her off before she could say any more. "Look, Sara," he said, "about what happened last night." But then he, too, halted, as if he weren't any more certain of what to say than she was.

"What?" she asked. "What about last night?"

He blew out a long, low breath, then pushed himself away from the door, covering the space between them in a few slow strides. When he stopped in front of her, he shoved his hands deep into the pockets of his trousers, as if he didn't quite trust himself not to touch her. Which was funny, Sara thought, because she didn't quite trust herself not to touch him, either. But—damn her luck—she didn't have pockets to retreat to.

"I guess I should apologize for what happened last night," he said, his expression earnest. "I guess I should tell you I'm sorry, and that it only happened because I was tired and not thinking straight."

"Should you?"

He nodded. "I should. But I won't. Because that would be lying."

Sara's heart began to thump madly then, and she crossed her arms fiercely over her midsection. She told herself to say something, but no words would come to her rescue. So she only continued to watch him in silence, hoping maybe he could clear it all up for both of them.

Evidently spurred by her lack of response, he continued. "I'm not sorry it happened. And I wasn't tired. I could have gone all night, and fully intended to. Hell, I was thinking straighter than I've ever thought about anything in my life when I kissed you. And dammit, I won't apologize for it."

Something wedged tight in her throat as he spoke, making it difficult for her to speak. All night with Shane... It was just too much to think about. Somehow, though, she managed to tell him, "I—I don't want you to...to apologize."

He eyed her warily. "You don't?"

She shook her head.

"But you're the one who called a stop to it," he reminded her.

"Yes."

"Because you didn't like it."

"No," she quickly assured him. "I didn't stop what was happening because I didn't like it."

He looked doubtful. "You didn't?"

She shook her head again.

"Then why did you stop?"

Go ahead, Sara, tell him. But even as she said it, she knew it would be a mistake. "I stopped because...because I liked it so much. Too much. I didn't want you to stop, Shane. Ever. And that's why I had to make myself—"

"Oh, Sara..."

And then, without warning, his arm was winding around her waist, and his lips were pressing into hers, and his fingers were threading through her hair at her temple, and the world was spinning out of control. Sara had no choice but to respond in kind, circling his lean waist with one arm to spread her hand open at the small of his back, curving her other hand over his warm nape, inhaling the clean, fresh scent of him as she opened her mouth beneath his.

And then he was inside her, or at least his tongue was, tasting her as deeply as he had the night before, and she felt her knees threatening to buckle. Desperately, she clung to him, fisting his shirt in her hand, gripping his shoulder as if to release him would mean letting go of life itself. Sensing her distress—or perhaps fearing she meant to pull away as she had the night before—he tightened his arm around her waist, jerking her more fiercely against him. Again and again he kissed her, slanting his head over hers, cupping his palm over the back of her head, bending her backward as he deepened the embrace even more. And still Sara held fast to him, because it wasn't nearly enough.

She knew what was happening, what *would* happen if she didn't put a stop to it right now. But where last night she hadn't been prepared to make love with Shane, tonight, strangely, she was. Maybe it was because they had survived the night, along with the kidnapping and the hijacking and everything else. Maybe she felt as if she wanted to reward herself—deserved a reward—for that. Or maybe it was because she didn't know what tomorrow would bring. Once they reentered the outside world, she feared that everything would go back to being the way it was before. And she didn't want that. She didn't know why she felt that way, only that she didn't want to go back to her life as it had been before. Before Shane Cordello. She wanted things to be different now. *She* wanted to be different. And she also wanted to have some good memories of this time with Shane to take with her, to temper the bad ones that might otherwise prevail.

She just wanted Shane, she conceded. Wanted him like she'd never wanted anything in her life. And where last night, there had been too many things that might have gone wrong, tonight everything seemed to have fallen into place. They were alone. They were comfortable. They were safe. Come morning, they would be rescued. And after that…

Well, Sara didn't want to think about after that. She only wanted to think about right now. And right now…

Oh, *right now*.

She tore her mouth from his, pushing her hands against his chest, to halt the onslaught of sensations and emotions, if only for a moment. By his expression, she knew he feared she was going to put a stop to their embrace again. So she smiled what she hoped was an encouraging smile, and cupped her palm gently over his cheek.

"I won't say, 'No,'" she promised. "And I won't say, 'Stop.'"

Relief filled his eyes, marred by puzzlement. "Then why…?"

"I just want to slow down a bit, that's all," she said. "I want us to take our time."

He grinned. "We can do that. For a little while. But then, Sara…"

"Then what?" she asked.

"Then I have plans for you, sweetheart."

Oh, my…

Instead of worrying about the fact that he knew infinitely more about what was happening between the two of them than she did, Sara focused on what she did have some knowledge about. Certainly she knew how to undress a man. It wasn't so frightfully different than undressing herself, was it?

She dropped her hands to the front of his shirt, flattening a palm on each side of his button placket. Immediately, though, she realized she had made a mistake. Undressing Shane would be completely different from undressing herself. Because what lay beneath his shirt was so utterly unlike what lay beneath hers. Even through the thin cotton fabric, she determined the strength and heat and hardness of him. And as she dragged her hands down his torso and back up again, she encountered bump after bump of rigid musculature. Another mistake, because in feeling the shape of him through his clothing, she discovered that she only wanted to know more.

With just a small hesitation, she lifted her hands to the uppermost button and, with great care, freed it from its mooring. She braved a glance up at Shane's face when she did so, and found that he was smiling at her…indulgently. Indulgently! Of all things. She wanted him to smile passionately. Wickedly. Wantonly. Not indulgently.

"See anything you like?" he asked with much amusement. Amusement! Of all things.

"Not yet," she said, growing bolder.

Feeling challenged now, she slowly freed the second, then the third button of his shirt. Little by little, she increased her speed and, one by one, unfastened all that were left. Then she dipped her hands below the garment, her intention to skim it right off of his shoulders without so much as a by-your-leave. But she halted the moment her hands connected with his body. He felt so…extraordinary. Solid and hard and strong, yet soft and velvety and limber. The dark hair growing across his chest drew her fingers in and, fascinated now, she took her time exploring him. She thumbed his flat nipples, tripped her fingers over his rigid abdominals, slid her thumb into the divot at the base of his powerful throat. She couldn't help herself—she found his physique so intriguing. Again and again, around and around, she let her hands explore him, marveling at all she encountered, until she had indeed pushed his shirt over his shoulders and he stood before her half-naked.

So surprised was she by her own gesture, and so enraptured had she become by all she'd discovered that she didn't realize what her exploration had done to Shane— until she glanced up at his face again and saw that all the passion, all the wickedness and all the wantonness she had hoped for was now indeed present. In spades.

She gasped as he pulled her hard against him, and her pulse accelerated wildly as he skimmed his hand lower, down over her shoulder blade, along her spine, to the small of her back, where he spread his fingers open wide. He dipped his head to hers again, capturing her mouth with his, tasting her with just the tip of his tongue, sliding it first along her upper lip, then slowly, oh so slowly, along the plump curve over her lower one. Then, as he nestled his mouth more resolutely over hers, he slipped his hand lower still, over the rounded arc of her bottom. Sara gasped at the contact, and he took advantage of her response by tasting her more deeply, thrusting his tongue into her mouth and pushing her entire body closer to his.

As he did, his fingers closed more intimately over her derrière, and she felt the heat of his palm warming her flesh through the thin cotton of her skirt. Hot, too, was the friction he created when he began to rub his hand over the fabric, dragging it over her sensitive, otherwise naked, flesh, searing her, scorching her, inside and out. She jerked her mouth away from his to gasp for breath, but he immediately reclaimed it, kissing her even more deeply than before, hauling her body fiercely against his own. She felt him swell and ripen against her belly, and she nearly fainted dead away at the sheer size and demand of him. She knew

enough about what happened between a man and a woman,
even if she'd never experienced it for herself. And it didn't
take an expert to realize that Shane Cordello would be a
formidable lover.

As if he sensed such a realization were forming in her
brain and he didn't want to disappoint her in her assump-
tion, he gripped her hand in his and pulled it between their
bodies, cupping her palm boldly over that part of himself.
Then he covered the back of her hand with his own palm
and pressed hard, urging both their fingers down along his
inflexible length. Then up again. Then down again, until
Sara feared she would lose consciousness at the demand
and intimacy in the action. But she had no desire to stop
it. He was so hard and long and solid, and she wondered
what it must feel like to invite such a man inside.

As she envisioned that happening, Shane began to take
further liberties, moving the hand on her bottom again,
lower still, to her thigh this time, where he grasped her
skirt tightly in his fist. As he continued to kiss her, each
more intense than the one preceding it, he began to drag
the garment upward, over her calves, her knees, her thighs,
until he had bared her bottom completely to the cool kiss
of the night air.

Oh, heavens, Sara thought wildly. Vaguely, she thought
once more about whether or not she should put a stop to
this before things went too far. Then she realized that things
had already gone too far. Much too far. No man had ever
touched her the way Shane seemed intent on touching her,
with no barrier between his flesh and hers. And then, before
she could speak, he *was* touching her, his whole, big hand
curving over the delicate skin of her behind.

"Oh, man," he groaned against her mouth as he touched
her. "I wondered if you'd be bare-assed, too. Oh, Sara…"

And then he was kissing her again, touching her, palming
and petting the soft globes of her bottom. He creased the
sensitive cleft with sure fingers, then he gave one buttock
an ungentle squeeze before driving one finger between

them again for a soft, scant penetration. Sara cried out at the shocking nature of the action, and at the even more scandalous sensations that rushed through her in response. Her entire body felt hot and liquid, as if she were about to burst into flames. She tried to tell him to stop, to put her skirt back in place, to let her go, that they were moving too quickly, but she couldn't make herself form the words to issue the order. Probably, she realized wildly, because she didn't *want* to form the words or issue the order. Because she wanted to keep feeling this way for as long as she possibly could.

Shane must have taken her feral little cry as encouragement—and indeed she couldn't say that it wasn't—because he dipped his other hand between their bodies and up under the fabric of her shirt in front. The waistband hung low on her hips, so he was able to trace the circle of her navel, then move upward, cupping her naked breast with sure fingers. He groaned again when he realized no barrier stood between him and his prize, gently kneading her flesh before closing his thumb and forefinger over the tumid peak. Over and over he teased her sensitive flesh, thumbing her, palming her, driving her nearly mad with wanting him.

When he ended their kiss with a savage gasp, she thought he only meant to draw air. But what he did was push her breast higher, outside the scooped neck of her blouse, then lower his head to pull her inside his mouth instead. He sucked as much of her in as he could, laving her first with the flat of his tongue, then taunting her with its tip. Again and again he tasted her, toyed with her, teased her, pushing her breast deep into his mouth with one hand as he fondled her bottom with the other.

And as he pleasured her that way, Sara gripped his shoulders hard in her hands, because she began to feel very faint indeed, and feared she might melt away if she didn't hang on tight. Her knees did buckle beneath her then, but Shane kept her aloft with his greedy, expert hands. And just when she was certain she would come apart at the seams, he upped the ante again, moving the hand on her fanny lower still, slipping his fingers between her legs, to that most torrid, clandestine part of her.

Oh, heavens…

Without warning, and without hesitation, he penetrated her deeply with one long finger, the first such invasion Sara had ever felt. She knew he didn't know that, knew he must think she was at least a little experienced when it came to sex. She knew she had to tell him the truth—that she'd never been with any man this way before. Because he had a right to know that. But she feared that if she told him, he would stop what he was doing. Or, at the very least, he would go slower. He would be more patient. He would stop doing the things to her that he was currently doing. And that was the last thing she wanted him to do.

Heaven help her, she couldn't tell him. She couldn't. Not if it meant he would stop touching her the way he was touching her now. Because the way he was touching her now was… Erotic. Hypnotic. Narcotic.

And still not nearly enough…

Nine

"Shane," Sara finally managed to gasp. "Shane, please." Though what she was pleading with him to do, she couldn't honestly say. Part of her wanted him to stop what he was doing, at least long enough for her to *think* about what was happening. But another larger, more insistent, part of her wanted to make him promise that he would never, ever stop, because she never wanted to have to think about anything again.

He must not have heard her, though, because he didn't slow his ministrations. In fact, he slid a second finger inside her, spreading the two digits, widening her, making her writhe with a need for something she couldn't even identify, and making it nearly impossible for her to keep standing.

"Oh, Shane," she tried again. "Please. Please, you have to—"

"What?" he interrupted her, the single word falling hotly and damply against her naked bosom. He traced the upper curve of her breast with the tip of his tongue, and she emitted another frantic sound from the back of her throat, a sound she didn't even recognize as coming from herself.

"We can't... You mustn't... I'm not... It isn't..."

"We can," he countered breathlessly. "I have to. You are. And it is. All of it, Sara. We need to do all of it."

"But—"

"Shh," he interrupted her. "Don't talk."

"But I—"

He cut her off. "Just feel." Then he deftly inserted a third finger inside her, flexing it with the other two, stimulating her in a way that made her entire body hum. "Just feel me," he whispered, the words coming right beside her ear. Only then did she realize that she had closed her eyes, so she hadn't seen him straighten and move his face closer to hers. "Feel me inside you," he murmured.

"I do," she whimpered, scarcely able to even manage those two small words.

"Oh, you're so tight," he gasped. "So sweet. It's going to be so good between us. I promise you, Sara. So good."

"Oh, Shane..."

"Feel what I do to you," he whispered, moving his fingers inside her once more. He moved his other hand to her bottom again, raking over the taut flesh again and again. "And think how it will feel when we're in bed, with you on top of me, and me going even deeper than this."

"Oh, Shane..."

"Think about it, Sara."

"I am. Oh, I *am*..."

At her heated declaration, he scooped her up into his arms and carried her over to the bed, depositing her at its center. She sensed, more than felt, him skimming the loose blouse off of her body, urging her backward so that he could remove her skirt, as well. She lifted her hips to facilitate her disrobing, but found that she could manage little other movement. Then she watched, still and silent, feeling drugged and disoriented, as he shed his shoes and trousers. She had been right in gauging him as *formidable,* she saw as the moonlight silvered the front of his body. He was magnificent, muscled, almost menacing somehow in his confidence. He knew what he wanted, and he knew what to do and say to get it. And Sara, heaven help her, wanted nothing more than to give it to him. Energy and intent seemed to hum from every cell in his body. And every cell in his body was absolutely glorious.

Without thinking about what she was doing, she extended her hand toward him in silent invitation. And Shane immediately accepted. He joined her on the bed, the tiny bed that commanded closeness, lying on his side beside her. He kissed her again, tracing a finger along all the curves and valleys of that one exposed side—over her jaw, her shoulder, her breast, the dip of her waist, the flair of her hip, her thigh. Then he pulled back again, taking her hand in his, and rolled over onto his back, tugging her along, atop him. Instinctively, Sara straddled his lean, hard torso, closing him within her bent knees. He smiled as he reached up to fill his hands with her breasts, thumbing the stiff peaks, rolling them between his fingers, tracing the ample circles of her areolae.

"You are so beautiful," he said softly.

The observation seemed not to invite a response, so final was his tone when he uttered it. So Sara only smiled at him in return, splaying her own hands open over the warm, hard satin of his chest, marveling at the musculature she had seen only on stone-carved Greek gods before now. He was beautiful, too, she thought. More beautiful than anything she had ever seen before.

He caressed her breasts for a few moments more, long enough to drive her to near lunacy, then shifted his hands down to her waist, settling them over the curve of each hip. Gently, he pulled her forward over his flat belly, an action Sara didn't expect, but one she found wildly erotic, as it generated a friction beneath her that was quite...extraordinary. Then, a bit less gently, he pushed her backward again, the friction more insistent this time, leaving a damp trail on his flesh in its wake. Sara was melting a little inside, floating on an aphrodisiac high, waiting for him to pull her forward on another slick ride, when, as if Shane recognized something she didn't, he lifted her upward and over him, then began to slide her down. And then, suddenly, he was parting her with his thick, heavy staff, breaching her, slowly penetrating her.

"We can start this way," he told her. "But I want to do it every way with you tonight, Sara. Every way we can imagine."

Oh, she could imagine some wonderful ways, so, almost delirious now, she only nodded.

"And I like it fast and hard," he added. "Is that okay with you?"

Not fully understanding what he meant, and frankly too far gone by now to care, Sara nodded again. She didn't want anything to interrupt the intensity of the pace they'd set, and "fast and hard" sounded extremely erotic. Shane smiled at her agreement, a wide, satisfied smile. She was about to smile back when, simultaneously, he jerked her body down hard over his and thrust his roughly against— and inside—her own.

The pain that shot through her then was quite distressing. And she was helpless not to cry out at the hot, knife-sharp paroxysm that sliced through her entire abdomen at his invasion. Shane must have realized at the same time that he had just violated a barrier no man had yet to penetrate, because after one stark moment inside her, he immediately withdrew and rolled her to her back, bracing himself over her on elbows he folded on each side of her.

"You're a *virgin?*" he cried in utter astonishment.

Still gasping at the spiral of pain that had wound briefly through her, Sara somehow managed a wry smile. Unable to help herself, she reached up to thread her fingers through his dark hair with much affection. Then, very softly, she said, "Well, not anymore, I'm not."

Shane studied her in absolute silence for a moment, unmoving, as if he had turned to stone. Then, "Oh, hell," he muttered. He, too, rolled over onto his back, his body still pressing into hers thanks to the smallness of the bed. Then he covered his eyes with one hand and repeated, "Oh, hell."

Sara bit her lip and somehow managed to hold back the tears she felt threatening. She tried to tell herself they were the result of the pain that had shot through her, and not due to Shane's carelessly offered words. Somehow, though, the latter hurt far worse than the former had.

"Was it really that ghastly?" she asked softly.

Immediately, Shane dropped his hand to the mattress and rolled to his side to look at her. "Of course not," he said. "But, Sara..."

"What?"

"You should have told me."

She studied him in silence for a moment, then, "If it was that important to you," she said, "then you should have asked me."

"But I just assumed—"

"Well, you shouldn't have."

He opened his mouth to respond to that, then closed it again. After a moment spent searching her face, he finally said, "You're right. I shouldn't have assumed you were... That you'd never... I mean..."

"What, you can't even say the word now?" she asked, injecting a playfulness into her voice she didn't feel. "My, this is a problem."

"No, I just mean..." He sighed heavily. "I shouldn't have assumed, that's all. Because now that I think about it, it all makes sense."

"What do you mean?" she asked.

"The fact that you're—that you *were*," he corrected himself with obvious reluctance, "a...you know."

"Virgin?" she supplied helpfully.

"Yeah. That."

"What, have I had a big white *V* pinned to my clothing we both overlooked somehow and it's just now becoming obvious?"

He shook his head. "No. But I still should have realized."

"How could you possibly have realized?" she asked. For some reason, she was beginning to feel a little irritated. What, was she so very different from other women? Was she too pure? Too chaste? Too innocent? Too naive? None of those words seemed particularly flattering in these modern times. And none of them felt appropriate to Sara at all. Just because she was—had been—a virgin, didn't mean she wasn't worldly. One could be sophisticated and knowledgeable without having *lost it,* so to speak.

Shane smiled at her, and some of her irritation fled at seeing it. It evaporated completely, though, when he told her, "Because you're not like any woman I've ever met before, that's how."

She decided to take that as a compliment, even if he didn't seem altogether happy when he said it. In fact, his smile grew decidedly melancholy as he spoke. In spite of that, she smiled, too. "You're not like any man I've ever met, either," she told him.

He said nothing in response to that for a moment, only searched her face in silence as if he were looking for the answer to a very important question. Finally he asked, "So now what happens?"

Sara turned on her side to face him. She might as well be honest, she thought. After all, she had nothing to lose. Oh, except perhaps for the most wonderful, amazing, arousing man she had ever met in her life. Somehow she made herself smile as she said, "Actually, I had rather hoped I might experience an orgasm at some point in the evening. From what I've heard, they do sound like frightfully good fun."

Shane stared at her in openmouthed silence for a moment, then laughed outright. "You mean you still want to…?"

This time Sara was the one to gape. "Well, don't you?"

"Of course I do, but…"

"But what?" she asked.

"But aren't you…?"

"What?"

"Hurting?"

Sara laughed, too, at that. "I won't lie to you, Shane. It did hurt like the very devil at first." She thumbed a lock of hair back from his forehead and tried to ignore the wealth of affection she felt bubbling up inside her. "But what would be more painful," she said, "is if we stopped just when things were beginning to go well."

He grinned. "Well, since you put it that way…"

Before she had a chance to respond to that, he reached for her again, pulling her atop him as she had been before. "Is that okay?" he asked. "Would you rather try something different?"

"Oh, yes," she said enthusiastically. "This is very okay. It's very exciting. And as soon as we've done it this way, I want to do it another way, too. And then I want to try something else. And then something else. And then some—"

He halted her by seizing her shoulders and pulling her down for a kiss that was even hungrier, needier and more demanding than before, then pushed her back up again.

"You," he said, "are a very sexy woman."

She grinned. "Even if I've never…"

He smiled, too, but it was that sad sort of smile he had used before. "Believe it or not, Sara, knowing this is your first time only makes it—only makes *you*—that much more exciting."

Well, since he put it like that…

"I'll be gentler this time," he said.

"Oh, damn," she replied, frowning.

He laughed. "Trust me, Sara. It'll be better that way at first. Maybe later—"

But he halted without finishing whatever he intended to say. Whether that was because he didn't want to frighten her or didn't want to think that far ahead, she couldn't tell. Maybe it was just that he didn't think there would be a later, that this might be their one and only chance to be together. As much as Sara hated to admit it, she halfway wondered that herself. Which, she supposed, was another reason why tonight she was so much more ready than she had been the night before. This might be their last chance to be together. And she didn't want to miss out on the opportunity to be with a man like Shane. Men like him, after all, only came along once in a lifetime.

"Make love to me, Shane," she said. "Please."

He obviously needed no other encouragement, because he settled his hands on her hips once again, more gently this time. But instead of urging her backward as he had before, he pulled her forward this time. Sara didn't protest, though she was confused by the action. Until he had pulled her up over his chest and scooted himself down some more. Until he gripped her hips and lifted her up off of him and urged her forward some more, over his mouth.

Before she had a chance to fully comprehend his intention, he pulled her down toward his face, against his mouth, and tasted her in a way that made her entire body catch fire. Instinctively, Sara gripped the wrought-iron headboard and rose up on her knees, but Shane followed, clutching her buttocks now, pushing her forward, flicking his tongue into all the places his fingers had made ready, spurring a hot river of wantonness to flood her. Again and again he savored her, relished her, feasted upon her, and with each new advance, Sara felt as if she would come apart inside. Little ripples of pleasure began to expand from her center, growing wider and stronger with each new push forward from Shane. She heard a low, feral sound and then realized she was the one making it. And then, a tiny little explosion detonated inside her. Followed by another. And another. And another…

And then she was coming apart inside, splintering into hundreds of little shards of delight. Every cell in her body seemed to hum with ecstasy, joining into one massive explosion of gratification. She cried out again, but this time it was sheer pleasure, and not pain, that generated the response.

And the next thing she knew, she was lying beneath Shane, her fingers tangled in his hair, her mouth pressed hotly to his, her legs wrapped over his thighs as if she intended to never let him go. And as he kissed her, he entered her again, more slowly this time, giving her a chance to become accustomed to his size and presence. Little by little, he drove himself farther into her, all the while kissing her, holding her, telling her how beautiful she was, how sexy she was, how incredibly lovely she was….

And then he was fully inside her, spreading her wide, and the discomfort Sara had felt initially gradually began to ebb. She felt full of him, as if he had overtaken her, and his dominion excited her beyond belief. Because she could see in his face that she held reign over him, as well. She wasn't the only one moved by their joining. Shane, too, seemed more than a little overwhelmed.

"You okay?" he asked raggedly when he had sheathed himself completely inside her.

She nodded weakly.

"No pain?"

She shook her head. "Nothing I can't handle."

"I don't want to hurt you, Sara."

"You won't."

"But—"

"Shh," she said softly, placing two fingers over his lips. "Just make love to me," she told him. "Please. Make me yours, Shane. Make me always remember this night. Make me never forget…"

As he moved inside her, she found she could no longer

speak, couldn't finish her sentence about never forgetting him. Slowly, methodically, he withdrew and reentered her, her slick canal hugging his heavy length. Again and again he moved into and out of her, increasing his pace and his depth with each thrust. At Sara's urging, he abandoned his tender entry for faster, more furious stroking, and she hooked her legs around his waist to pull him deeper still. And then, once again, she began to feel the little ripples of delight spiraling through her. This time, though, they came with a power and a fury they hadn't before. This time, when Sara cried out, it was in union with Shane, something that made their responses to each other all the more volatile.

And then, as quickly as the eruption had come, it began to ebb. He relaxed against her, rolling to his side and bringing her with him, their bodies still joined. He folded both arms across her bare back, thrusting a hand into her hair at her nape. He pulled her close and kissed her temple with utter sweetness, something that seemed even more intimate than the coupling they had just shared. Then he moved far enough away to gaze at her face, saying nothing, looking into her eyes as if he were once again looking for the answer to some age-old question.

Sara wished she knew how to respond. But all she could manage was to lift a hand to his face and trace his full mouth with trembling fingertips. Then she kissed the lips her fingers had touched and lay her head on the pillow. The last thing she remembered was hearing Shane say her name. And then he said something else, too, but she was just too sleepy to hear it....

Dawn came way too early as far as Shane was concerned, even though, when he awoke, it was to find his senses overflowing with Sara. He lay on his side, his arm draped over her rosy, naked body, fitted so perfectly against his own, his hand filled with her warm, luscious breast. When he inhaled, he smelled her, all sweet and musky and womanly, and when he opened his eyes to the faint morning light, he saw her face in profile on the pillow beside his, all elegant lines and graceful beauty. As he watched her, she murmured quietly in her sleep, echoing so many of the erotic sounds she'd uttered the night before, and Shane went hard against her bottom. He remembered how intoxicating she had tasted and, unable to resist, he dipped his head and brushed his lips along her cheek.

She woke slowly, turning her head back toward his, and he moved forward to cover her mouth, kissing her more ardently this time. She murmured another soft sound of pleasure as she kissed him back, reaching one hand lazily behind herself to weave her fingers through his hair. He in turn reached forward, pressing his hand over her naked belly, then down between her legs. She parted them willingly, and he dipped his fingers into her nest of curls, stroking and plowing her until she was damp with desire. He continued to pet her as he pushed himself deep inside her from behind, shoving his hips forward even as she pressed hers back. For long moments, they clung to each other, their mouths locked in a fierce union, Shane pumping gently but swiftly in and out of her. With one final forward thrust, he emptied himself into her one last time, and then both of them lay trembling, back to front, until the sun rose fully over the horizon.

And as whiter light bled over the windowsill, brightening the room and hastening their departure, Shane wished he knew what the hell they were supposed to do now.

Had he told her last night that he loved her? He couldn't remember now. He thought he might have said the words he'd never once uttered to a woman, but now it seemed a hazy misconception. If he had said them, had he meant them? Oh, surely not, he told himself now. Sometimes a person said something in the throes of passion he might not say otherwise. And man what passion they'd been thrown into the night before. He couldn't remember ever having such a shattering experience with a woman. Never in his life had he felt the things he'd felt last night with Sara. And she'd been a—

Oh, jeez, that was another thing. A virgin. He'd never bedded a virgin before. Virgins were just really tricky. They tended to take first times way too seriously. They tended to think of the men involved in those first times as special. The last thing Shane wanted to be for any woman was special. But then, Sara wasn't just any woman, was she? No, she was— He swallowed hard when he realized. She was special.

Oh, hell. What was he supposed to do now?

Neither seemed to know what to do at that point, because they rose and washed and dressed in an awkward silence. Neither seemed any more inclined to look at the other than they did talk to the other, because they were as good about avoiding each other's gazes as they were each other's words. Maybe it was better if they didn't talk about it, he thought. Not yet. There would be time later, he promised himself. Time for them to sort everything out once they got to Penwyck.

When they made their way downstairs, they found that Hilda had fixed breakfast for the four of them. They made quiet small talk—or, rather, Sara and the Santoses made quiet small talk, since Shane couldn't begin to think of anything to say himself—and then Enrique offered to drive them to the nearest town, Maria Lupe.

The drive, too, took place mostly in silence, with only a few words exchanged between Sara and their host. Enrique dropped them off in front of the local police station, assuring them, she said through her translation, that the local constabulary would be most helpful about finding the bandits who had overtaken them in the mountains. When she and Shane climbed out of the car and said their goodbyes, Enrique thrust his hand out of the driver's side window. As he shook Shane's, he pressed some money into his palm, which Shane accepted guiltily, suspecting it had been hard-won by the elderly couple. Then their host wished them well and waved goodbye.

And then, once again, Sara and Shane were on their own, neither having a clear idea what to do next.

By mutual agreement, they turned their backs on the police station once Enrique was out of sight. Then, after a brief glance up one side of the street and down the other, they began to make their way toward a hotel that seemed to be the centerpiece for the town square. It made up one side of a small, green, parklike setting, with little shops and cafés hugging the other sides. Shane felt certain they would find a public telephone inside.

"I, um, I wrote down the Santoses' address before we left so we can pay them back when we get to Penwyck," he said, jingling the change Enrique had given him with the paper money as they made their way down the street. "I guess right now we should call someone, though."

Sara nodded. "Yes, of course. I'll contact the RII immediately and they can tell the RET where we are."

"The RET?" Shane asked. "Now who the hell are they?"

She seemed relieved by the bland subject matter, because she managed a slight smile—of clear relief. "The RET is part of the RII," she clarified. "It stands for Royal Elite Team. The cream of the crop, so to speak. They're essentially the king's right-hand men. They direct covert operations and rescues and such. But it will be members of the RII who actually come to fetch us."

"Sounds like an interesting group," Shane said.

"Yes, they are, actually. As I said, my father worked for them," she added, almost as an afterthought. "And I have a job waiting there myself once I graduate in the spring."

Aha, Shane thought. That explained a lot about how Miss Pink Sweater had become Miss Butt Kicker.

"The RII will be the ones who've been handling our disappearance," she continued. "It should make their jobs easier now that they won't have to come beating through the brush to look for us.''

Shane nodded toward the hotel. ''There's probably a pay phone inside,'' he said. And rooms, too, he thought further, seeing as how it would probably take the RII at least a couple of hours to get to them once they were called and maybe he and Sara could use that time to—

''Yes, of course,'' she said, extending her hand toward him.

For a moment, Shane let himself believe she wanted him to take her hand in his and lead her to one of those hotel rooms where they could make a quick phone call and have a not-so-quick tumble. Then he made himself acknowledge that she just wanted the money he held, so he passed it to her. He also realized, much to his surprise, that he didn't want to get a room so that the two of them could make love again. No, really, all he wanted to do with Sara in a quiet room was talk. About everything that had happened. About what they were going to do now. About what would happen once they arrived in Penwyck. And not just with the potential-missing-heir-to-the-throne thing, either.

''Thanks,'' she said softly as she took the money from him…and, as she had since that morning, avoided his gaze.

Then she spun around and made her way up the stairs toward the hotel, leaving Shane nothing to do but follow. It was an antique building, to be sure, but grand, three stories high, and looking like a big, white, old-world palace. Hotel Magnífico, it said in scrolling letters over the dark green awnings that spanned each of the first-story windows. Shane couldn't possibly disagree.

The inside was as charming as the outside, with pale pink stucco arches, and marble floors dotted with potted palms taller than Shane, and Oriental rugs that were splashed with muted tones. He almost felt as if he'd just stepped onto the set of *Casablanca*.

They located a phone in an alcove off the lobby that was partially obscured by some of those man-size palms, and

Sara set about dialing. He knew there was little chance the Black Knights were lurking around, but he kept his back to her as she waited for a response, scanning the hotel lobby in search of suspicious characters and the usual suspects. But the place seemed harmless—not to mention pretty deserted—so he turned an ear to the conversation Sara began behind him. Unfortunately, he could only hear her side of it. But what he heard pretty much let him know that she was getting chewed out. Royally.

"Yes, I realize that, sir," she was saying apologetically. "But you have to understand that… What? Yes, but… I know, but… But you see, sir, it wasn't… I know that, but… But there wasn't any time to… But I had no way of knowing that…." She sighed heavily in defeat and, for several moments, surrendered to the angry male voice buzzing through the line.

Shane could only imagine what it must be costing her to stay silent, and he made a promise to himself to let the big boys of the RII know she'd done all she could with what she'd had to work with. Not that she'd probably welcome his intervention, because he'd seen for himself that she liked to do things her way, but he'd do it anyway.

And then what? a little voice piped up at the back of his head.

I'll think about that later, he immediately replied.

Because, hey, that was Shane's philosophy when it came to things of a personal, i.e. romantic, nature: Why do today what you could put off until tomorrow? Then again, if he'd put off making love to Sara until tomorrow he never would have known how incredible the two of them would be together.

Yeah, said the voice. *And you wouldn't be standing here not knowing what the hell you're supposed to do, either.*

Yeah, yeah, yeah, Shane thought. He was about to say something snippy to the voice when Sara began to talk again, and he returned his attention to what she was saying.

"As I tried to tell you, sir," she began again, "I had

little reason to think that was a possibility. I was told this was going to be a routine assignment, escorting Mr. Cordello to Penwyck. And I've nearly got him there,'' she added. ''If you can just send someone to Maria Lupe, Spain, we'll be waiting in the lobby of the Hotel Magnífico, which is two blocks east of the police station on Calle Norte. How soon can you have someone here? Oh, lovely. Yes, we'll be fine until then. Thank you. We'll be waiting in the bar.''

Or a room, Shane wanted to say. They could get a room instead. Hey, why take chances, right?

Before he could make the suggestion, however, Sara hung up the phone with ferocity, then growled under her breath and spun around to lean against the wall. Evidently her altercation with her superior had squashed whatever discomfort she'd felt being with Shane, because now she spoke readily and to his face.

''What a stupid git,'' she said. ''They act like I did this on purpose. As if I wanted the two of us to be hijacked and kidnapped and imprisoned. Oh, yes. There's nothing I enjoy more than running through the brush during the cold night with no provisions and a big gorilla hot on my trail.''

Shane forced a smile. ''And even though I did that stick thing I promised, you never even invited me up for a nightcap,'' he said.

She sobered at that, meeting his gaze levelly. ''I am truly sorry to have gotten you into this,'' she said. ''Had I suspected for a moment that the Black Knights would try something like this, I never—''

''You don't owe me an apology, Sara,'' Shane interrupted. ''What happened wasn't your fault.''

''But it was, don't you see?'' she objected. ''I was entrusted to bring you safely back to Penwyck, and I failed miserably.''

''You didn't fail,'' he said. ''You're taking me safely back to Penwyck. It's just going to take a little longer than we thought, that's all.''

She shook her head. "No, I won't be taking you safely back to Penwyck," she said softly. "The RII will."

Oh, now that didn't sound good at all. "What do you mean?"

"Not surprisingly, they tracked us very well," she said. "They have operatives working right here in Maria Lupe, and they've already apprehended two of the kidnappers. Alas, Fawn and the other are still eluding them, but perhaps with our help, those two will be rounded up shortly, as well. But the RII agents will be here momentarily. They've been working with the local police and are right up the street. And they'll be escorting you back to Penwyck today. They'll hand you over personally to Queen Marissa in just a few hours, I imagine."

"But you—"

"I'll stay here for a debriefing and return to Penwyck shortly," she finished for him. "I'm sure Admiral Monteque himself will want to talk to me. If for no other reason than to tell me what a failure I am," she muttered in conclusion, not quite under her breath.

Her expression changed not one iota as she told him all of this, but Shane knew she wasn't nearly as calm and collected as she was letting on. Her eyes were too bright, her chin too fiercely angled, her mouth too grim. She was no happier about this development than he was. Though for her, he had to admit, it might just have been because her career was in trouble, and not necessarily because she wanted to stay with Shane.

No, he immediately contradicted himself. Oh, sure, her job was on the line, but that wasn't the only thing upsetting her. "Sara—" he began.

"Everything will be fine, Shane," she said, cutting him off. "In a few hours, you'll be with your brother and the queen, and you can get this switched-at-birth thing settled once and for all and move on with your life. Whatever direction it winds up taking."

"But you—"

"And I'll be able to move on with my life, as well," she said before he had a chance to finish. "Whatever direction *it* winds up taking."

In other words, Shane translated, *It's over between us.*

And in realizing that, he felt like a Mack truck had just mowed him down. How could she say that? he wondered. How could she even suggest that the two of them should just go on with their lives after what had happened last night? After everything that had happened this week?

Well, what did you expect, Cordello? that annoying voice piped up again. *It's not like the two of you made any promises to each other. You sure as hell never made any to her.*

But that was only because he hadn't had the chance, he told the voice. When was he supposed to have made promises? While they were being hijacked? While they were being kidnapped? While they were being held for ransom? While they were running for their lives?

How about when you made love to her? the voice asked. *That might have been a good time.*

Had he told her he loved her? he wondered again. He honestly couldn't remember now. If he had, it certainly hadn't been with any real conviction. Certainly Sara offered no indication that he'd said anything to her then.

But he hadn't made any promises to her, that *was* certain. Not even when he'd realized he was the first man she'd allowed inside—literally and figuratively. Last night had to have been important to her, he thought. She wouldn't have made love with him if she hadn't cared. She wasn't the kind of woman to hold on to her virginity and then give it away carelessly to some guy who wasn't going to stick around. Shane had realized that even as he accepted her gift last night. In doing so, he had acknowledged, whether consciously or not, that he knew she cared for him. A lot.

But he'd said nothing to her to make her think he felt the same way, had offered her no indication that last night had meant anything more to him than other nights—with other women—had. Even an avowal of love could be mis-

construed. People said things when they made love. That
didn't mean they meant them. Even if Shane *hadn't* ever
said those words to any other woman before. Sara had no
real reason to think he wanted her to stay around. And this
was her way of letting him off the hook.

"Sara—" he began again.

"Oh, look," she interrupted him again, "they've broken
their own record. They're here already."

She was looking at something over his shoulder, so
Shane turned to follow her gaze. He saw two middle-aged
men dressed in what might have passed for vacation wear
on other men: loose-fitting linen trousers and pastel-colored
guayabera shirts. But the government-issue sunglasses and
the listening devices each wore in his ear sort of spoiled
the image. It took them no time to locate Sara and Shane,
and they moved swiftly and with much purpose across the
lobby toward them.

"Wallington," the first man said as they approached, his
voice completely lacking inflection, "we'll take it from
here. Morrisey is waiting for you outside in the car."

Sara nodded with clear resignation, then turned to Shane.
"Good luck," she said blandly. "I hope everything works
out the way you hoped it would." And although her voice
may have been empty when she spoke, her eyes...

Oh, God, her eyes, Shane thought. They were filled with
regrets and wants and needs that he wished like hell he
could stay and repair. There was so much he wanted to tell
her in that moment, so much he wished he'd said the night
before. But he couldn't say those things now. Not with two
strangers looking on. Not when Sara's career might have
been jeopardized with what he had to say.

"Be happy," she told him.

As if that would be possible without her, he thought. But
all he said in response was, "Yeah, thanks."

And then he was being escorted across the lobby and out
the door, where not one, but two, nondescript, British-
manufactured sedans idled at the curb. The back door of

one swung open in a ghostly fashion, and one of Shane's escorts directed him inside before following. The other man took a seat in the front, and a woman drove them away. He turned to look out the back window and saw Sara climbing into the back seat of the other car, but not before she glanced one last time in his direction. Without thinking, he lifted a hand in farewell, even though he wasn't sure if she would see him. But he thought she smiled sadly before she crawled inside the other vehicle.

And then, just like that, Sara was gone.

Ten

The palace at Marlestone, Penwyck's capital and largest city, surpassed even what Shane had been sure were his own wildly exaggerated misconceptions. Even the city surpassed his expectations. He'd never traveled outside the United States, but he'd seen enough James Bond movies in his time to have a grasp on most of the major European capitals. Seeing Europe in person, however, he realized what a grave disservice he'd done in picturing the Old World way of life. As he and his RII companions drove through the streets of Marlestone, he saw that the city was aged like a fine antique, elegant and regal and distinguished, loaded with character and much like what he'd seen of London on the screen—only bigger and more three-dimensional. And where he'd figured the palace at Marlestone would be grand and refined, it was actually glorious and opulent.

As the car made its way through vast wrought-iron gates that were opened by formally attired guards, Shane saw that the palace bore little resemblance to a castle with moats and turrets and a drawbridge, and instead looked more like a massive stately home. Three stories high, the gray limestone gleamed in the early-afternoon sun, its scores of windows glittering like fine gems. An immense stone reproduction of the family crest was fastened on an arching vault at the center of the building's front, and the vast arching doorway reached nearly to the second floor.

Must be one hell of a foyer, he thought. Then again, why was he surprised? It was one hell of a palace, too. As a construction worker, he could only admire the craftsmanship and skill and hard labor that had obviously gone into creating such a structure. Especially since he'd been told that the main part of the place had been built more than four hundred years ago.

The car rolled to a halt at the front entrance, and a half-dozen people stepped forward to meet it. Shane searched the faces to see if one belonged to his brother, but everyone was a stranger. Introductions flew as he was hurried into the palace, and although Shane caught none of the names, he noted some of the titles, especially of the men and women associated with the RII. One woman was attached to the queen somehow, and a man, Shane thought, was one of her advisers. Frankly, his head was buzzing with information overload by then, so he only followed where they directed him.

Gradually, he lost much of his entourage, until only a group of four people escorted him through the innards of the palace. None were the RII agents who had accompanied him from Maria Lupe, however. Still, all of his current companions seemed to be of the same worker-bee level as the others, because none expressed or exuded any kind of authority. Which probably meant they were taking Shane to the people who did have authority, when the only person he really wanted to see was Sara. Or his brother. Someone who could help keep him grounded when he felt like everything around him was flying apart.

As he was led through what seemed like dozens of rooms and down dozens of corridors, past dozens of pieces of lavish furniture and paintings of dead nobility, Shane could only shake his head in wonder that there were people on the planet who actually lived this way. And the realization that there was some small possibility that he and Marcus might very well have been born to it, that, in other circumstances, they might very well have spent their entire lives in these very glorious, opulent surroundings was just...

Well, kind of gross, actually, Shane thought. Hell, the last kind of life he wanted was one like this—filled with material excesses and unearned privilege and bowing and scraping from the general population. After all, he'd gone out of his way to avoid a life like this.

Oh, he *could* have grown up in a situation like this. Okay, not *quite* like this, he conceded, as he and Marcus wouldn't have been princes or living in a palace. But their mother and father had been very wealthy when they were kids. The house on Chicago's Gold Coast that Shane recalled from his early childhood had, in many ways, been a minipalace, so ostentatious had both of his parents been. Their lifestyle had been that of the idle rich—he and Marcus had attended a posh private school and mixed with all the right families and they'd had anything and everything their little hearts desired. Except, of course, two parents who loved each other.

But even after the divorce, when Shane had been split up from his twin, his life had continued in much the same fashion. His mother had remarried six months later, to a man very much like her first husband—wealthy, well connected, idle, willing to do anything for a buck. Although they had moved from Chicago to upstate New York, Shane's lifestyle hadn't changed at all. He'd still lived in a minipalace and attended the best schools and run around with boys from other rich families. He'd still been given everything he wanted, whether he worked for it or not. He'd still missed his parents' involvement in his life.

Things had been the same with his second stepfather. And his third.

In fact, by the time Shane graduated from prep school, he was on the fast track to becoming a man just like the men who had raised him: wealthy, well connected, idle. And corrupt, too, because most of his mother's husbands after his father had been men who hadn't cared where their money came from or how it appeared, so long as it was at their disposal in great piles. Few had worked for a living. None had cared about anything other than themselves—and their money—which had become evident every time one of Shane's mother's marriages failed. The male role models he'd had throughout his life had left a lot to be desired. Oh, they'd been rich, to be sure. But they hadn't much been human. Certainly not the kind of human that Shane wanted to be.

Fortunately, he had been smart enough to realize that early on, and he'd made a pact with himself not to become one of them. Marcus had helped keep him centered, even though Marcus, too, grew up in the lap of luxury. Marcus had even worked hard to make sure he *stayed* rich and moved in the right circles to the point where he'd made his first million in real estate at the age of nineteen. But that had been the point—Marcus had *worked*. Marcus had *earned* his wealth. He hadn't rested on what he had and let others do the work for him. Marcus had taken the initiative.

So Shane had, too. Unfortunately, Shane didn't have his brother's head for business. Nor, truth be told, had he wanted it. Shane had always liked working with his hands, had liked performing physical labor more than mental tasks. And when he'd walked away from his mother's lifestyle and journeyed into his own, he hadn't really missed the riches and privilege. There had been something uniquely gratifying about making his own way in the world. For the first time in his life, he'd felt proud of himself, satisfied with himself. He'd felt useful and purposeful and important. The first time he'd completed a construction job, and watched the building rise from ground to the sky, he'd felt an enormous sense of pride. He had a physical manifestation of his hard work, and it was one that would provide scores of other people with shelter.

Whatever Shane had in his life, he'd earned it. All by himself. Working with his own two hands. And that made him feel proud. It made him feel worthy. It made him feel like he made an important contribution to the human race. Walking through the palace at Marlestone, however...

Well, all Shane felt was uncomfortable. There was too much wealth here, in his opinion. Too much privilege. And none of it had been earned by the Penwyck family, other than being born to it. Which, okay, was probably perfectly acceptable in this country, but to his own way of thinking, hard work provided far greater rewards.

After what felt like days of walking, Shane and his escorts finally halted by a door on the second floor of the palace. He assumed it would lead him to the throne room, or wherever the hell kings and queens did their business. Instead, he entered what looked like a bedroom—a really big, really luxurious bedroom—and his brother, Marcus, was standing by the window on the other side.

"Shane!" he exclaimed by way of a greeting when he spun around at the sound of the opening door.

As usual, Marcus's dark brown hair managed to look both shaggy and stylish, and his green eyes were lit with genuine happiness. Likewise, as usual, he was dressed in a dark power suit, a discreetly patterned silk tie knotted at his throat. The entire ensemble had probably set him back more than Shane made in a month, he couldn't help thinking with much amusement. At five-foot-ten, Marcus was a couple of inches shorter than Shane, but he carried himself in such a way as to make himself seem actually taller.

"It's about time you got here!" he added as he hurried across the room to pull his brother into a fierce hug. "I was so worried about you. Thank God you're all right."

Shane embraced Marcus gratefully, laughing as he did

so, slapping his brother's back a few times for good measure. "Sorry it took me so long," he said as they pulled apart. "I got a little distracted."

"By the Black Knights, no less, from what I hear. That group has caused more trouble to this country lately. You're lucky you made it out with your shirt."

Actually, Shane wanted to say, the Black Knights hadn't been the biggest distraction. That, of course, had been Sara Wallington. And he really didn't want to comment on the part about making it out with his shirt. Seeing as how he hadn't. But that was a story best saved for later, when the two brothers were alone and could share everything they'd both been through over the last couple of weeks. Shane especially wanted to hear more about the new woman in Marcus's life. He'd received a call from his brother a couple of weeks before the one that had led him to Penwyck, and the conversation then had been cryptic at best. Now, of course, Shane knew that Marcus had uncovered the strange details surrounding their births at that time, but just hadn't known what to tell his brother. And the woman in Marcus's life, Lady Amira Corbin of Penwyck, had been the one to fill in those pieces.

She'd also set Marcus on his ear, Shane had realized during that conversation. But his brother had been evasive about Amira during his last call, before Shane left L.A., and had instead focused on the royal twin-swapping escapade. As soon as the opportunity arose, however, he intended to pin Marcus down once and for all about the lady.

"It was, without question, the worst flight of my life," Shane agreed. "And the food wasn't very good, either. So what the hell has been going on here, anyway?"

Hastily, Marcus filled him in on what had been happening in Penwyck since the royal jet had been hijacked, about the ransom call the queen had received, demanding an end to the alliance with Majorco in exchange for the safe return of the possible future monarch. While Her Majesty had stalled for time, the RII had set about trying to follow the hijackers' trail from where the royal jet had last been tracked on radar. They'd managed to make it as far as Maria Lupe in Spain, but the trail had gone cold there, until they'd received Sara's call early that morning.

"Pretty lucky being kidnapped with a woman who's studying to become a member of the RII," Marcus observed. "But then, you've always been the lucky one, haven't you?"

That, Shane thought, was a topic of debate, depending on one's point of view. To his own way of thinking, though, yes, in this case at least, Shane had definitely been the lucky one. And not because Sara had been an aspiring member of the RII, either. But simply because Sara had been Sara.

"Look, do you know what happened to her? Where they took her?" Shane asked his brother. "Because I really need to talk to her."

Marcus shrugged. "I imagine she's with the RII, telling them about what happened. They want to talk to you, too, of course, but Queen Marissa has insisted she see you at once. And only after you've had a chance to freshen up. I told them to bring you here, to my room, so I could see you first."

Shane expelled a long, exasperated breath. "Oh, man, we have got so much to talk about," he said. "But right now, all I want to do is sleep for about ten weeks."

"You can't," Marcus told him. "You're scheduled for a command performance for Queen Marissa." He glanced down at his—very expensive—gold watch. "In about twenty minutes, as a matter of fact. And it's going to take us ten minutes to get to her room because she's in the opposite wing of the palace."

Shane blew out another weary sigh and picked at his shirt. "All right. But at least let me get out of these clothes. I hate plaid."

Marcus laughed. "I anticipated that," he said. He jutted a thumb over his shoulder, toward another door. "They put you in the room next to mine, right through that door. You have everything you need in there. I did some shopping for you when I heard you were on your way back to Penwyck. Levi's, Shane," he added meaningfully. "Button fly. Do you know how hard it is to find those in Penwyck? But Amira knew just where to go."

"Yes, let's talk about Amira when we have a chance, okay?" Shane asked with much interest and a big smile.

Marcus smiled back, and it was the smile of a man who had just uncovered the greatest treasure of all. And seeing as how Marcus was one of the wealthiest men in the world, that must have been some treasure. "I want you to meet her later," he said. "She's incredible, Shane. I never thought I'd meet a woman like her."

Shane's smile grew broader, and he felt the first ripples of genuine happiness he'd felt since... Well, since that morning with Sara, he realized. "So, then I should be preparing myself to wear a tuxedo here before long?" he asked, joking.

But much to his surprise, Marcus nodded in response.

Holy cow, Shane thought. He really had only been joking when he said that, since Marcus had never shown any more inclination toward getting married than Shane had. But here was Marcus, talking about a wedding as if it were the natural next step with the woman in his life.

"Are you serious?" Shane asked. "You're really getting married?"

Marcus nodded again. "And look, I know you break out in hives just at the thought of putting on anything other than denim, but just this once, bro? For me?"

Shane shook his head, smiling even more. "Yeah, yeah, yeah. If it'll make you happy."

"Actually, Amira is the one who'll make me happy," Marcus said, beaming. "But I'd still appreciate it if you'd wear a tux when you're my best man."

"For you, Marcus, anything."

And he damned well expected his brother to do likewise for him when it came time for Shane's wedding.

Whoa. Hold up there. Rewind.

Shane's wedding? Now there were two words he'd never expected to find used in the same zip code. By anyone, least of all himself. Yet here he'd just thought the phrase in his own head as if it were the most natural thing in the world for him to think about, too—and without any sort of provocation or threat being used. Amazing. What was even more amazing was that where just a week ago he would have been terrified by the merest suggestion of such a thing, now, suddenly, it didn't seem scary at all. In fact, it seemed kind of—

Oh, man. Oh, man, oh, man, oh, man.

"Shane?"

His brother's voice halted whatever further thoughts he might have had on the subject of weddings, his own or anyone else's, because he realized Marcus must have been speaking at length, and he'd heard not one word of what the other man had said.

"What?" Shane asked. "Did you say something?"

Marcus laughed, but there was something anxious in the sound. "Guess being kidnapped does sort of make a person a little distracted for a while. I told you you might want to change clothes before you meet Queen Marissa. Put on the suit I bought you, and save the blue jeans for later. There are certain rules to be followed in this country, and you don't wear jeans to meet the queen."

Rules, Shane thought. He wondered if maybe that was why Sara had balked at the idea of the two of them being together. Her grace and refinement suggested she had grown up among the wealthy class, and when he considered the way she'd dressed—his bandages had been pure silk, and designer to boot, he reminded himself—there was every reason to believe she was still thriving in those upper echelons of society. And Shane had made no bones about his own very working-class existence. Still, she didn't seem like the kind of woman who would let superficialities like that stand in the way. Then again, Shane had given her no reason to think there was a "way" to stand in front of.

Too much to think about right now, and not enough time to do it, that was his problem. He pushed all thoughts of Sara aside, promising he'd mull it all over later when he was alone, and talk it all out later with Marcus. To his brother, he said, "Yeah, I'm ready to meet the queen. Just give me a few minutes to clean up."

The queen's receiving room was in keeping with the rest of the palace—lush, lavish, opulent, sumptuous, extravagant and every other word you might find in a thesaurus if you looked up the word *luxurious*. The queen, however, struck Shane as being very no-nonsense. She appeared to be in her early fifties, was of medium height and slender build. She was a striking woman with her dark hair carefully arranged in some kind of bun, and penetrating blue eyes that seemed to see straight inside a person. Her attire, too, was no-nonsense—a plain navy blue dress with a discreet gold pin affixed to its collar, matching gold earrings in her ears and flat navy shoes on her feet.

It was almost, Shane thought, as if she were doing her best not to stir up controversy with her personal appearance. And succeeding very well, as far as he was concerned.

She stood near an ornate desk tucked into the corner of the room, flanked by a group of people whose functions Shane could only guess at. Various heads of state and secret-police types, he thought, only half-joking. Certainly they all looked to be of a serious bent.

"Mr. Cordello, we meet at last," Queen Marissa said, smiling warmly, but formally, as she approached him.

Shane stood where he was, but bowed as she drew nearer, because that was what Marcus had told him he was supposed to do. He also waited to see if she would extend her hand, because Marcus had told him to do that, too—to not offer to shake hands unless she did so first. She did, and Shane took her hand in his. Instead of shaking, though, she only gave his fingers a brief, subtle squeeze before dropping his hand. Then she gestured toward a long, ox-blood leather sofa near the fireplace, where a small fire provided more ambience than warmth.

"Please do sit down," she told him. "You and your brother both." At this, Marcus joined Shane on the sofa, seating himself on the other side from the queen. "I am anxious to hear about your experiences with the Black Knights," she continued, "but I know that the RII insist on speaking to you about that first."

She lifted a hand with two fingers slightly extended, and immediately, she was surrounded by a quartet of men dressed in a variety of business suits and military uniforms. They hovered around the opposite arm of the sofa, none standing more than a foot away from Her Majesty, as if they were intent on guarding her with their lives, even in her own private domain. Queen Marissa seemed not to notice their arrival, didn't even turn around to see if they were there, as if she took for granted the fact that they would be. And, of course, they were.

"In fact, I'd like to introduce you to some of the higher-ranking members of the Royal Elite Team," the queen went on, "who will want to be present during your interview with the RII. Admiral Monteque, Colonel Prescott, Sir Selwyn Estabon and His Grace Carson Logan."

Each of the men nodded in acknowledgment as the queen spoke his name, and Shane immediately forgot who was who and which was which, so profound was his nervousness about this entire meeting. So he greeted them as a group when he said, "Hello."

That single word was evidently the only encouragement the men needed, because they immediately launched into questions Shane had thought would come later, during his more formal interview with the RII.

"Mr. Cordello, can you give us a physical description of

the two Black Knights who hijacked Her Majesty's jet and are still at large?''

"Could you possibly find the house again, Mr. Cordello, where you and Miss Wallington were held captive, if given the opportunity to do so? It could provide some useful clues.''

"Did you hear any of the Black Knights say anything suspicious, Mr. Cordello, anything at all?''

"Did any of them perhaps mention diamonds, by any chance, Mr. Cordello? Or a diamond-smuggling operation? That's how they're financing their treasonous activities, you know.''

"Gentlemen!'' the queen interjected in a voice that brooked absolutely no argument. Immediately the questions ceased, and the men relaxed their aggressive postures. "There will be time later for you to speak with Mr. Cordello,'' she told them. "Right now, I wish to speak with him myself.''

But instead of speaking, she studied him intently in silence for a moment, gazing first at his eyes, then his nose, then his mouth and then back again. She seemed to be looking for something specific in his countenance, and Shane had no idea what to do except sit still and let her do it. Then she turned her attention to Marcus and inspected his face with the same scrutiny. And then, for several moments, her gaze flew between Shane and Marcus, as if she were trying very hard to discern something very important.

"It is clear,'' she finally said, "that the two of you are indeed brothers. Your resemblance to each other is remarkable. However, I see no hint of Penwyck heritage in either of you.'' She sighed mildly, her features softening. "But perhaps that is only because I don't wish to see a hint of Penwyck heritage. The thought that you might be my sons, and that this is the first time I've met you…'' Her voice trailed off. "Well, I just can't accept that it might be true. My sons…'' She halted again, then shook her head, as if she had imparted much too personal an observation. "We shall perform the DNA tests as soon as possible," she said. "And we shall let that be the deciding factor."

"If it's any help, Your Majesty," Shane said quietly, "I don't think we're your sons, either. It just doesn't..." Now it was his voice that trailed off. "It just doesn't feel right," he finally said. "No offense, ma'am."

She smiled. "None taken, I assure you."

He had opened his mouth to say something else, though, honestly, Shane wasn't sure what he could say that might make the situation less awkward, when, without warning, the door to the queen's receiving room crashed open, framing a woman who was very attractive, and looked to be in her twenties. She also very much resembled the queen with dark hair that was pulled back from her face, and in the shape of her eyes—though they were green instead of Her Majesty's blue. The woman was also clearly pregnant, and dressed in a simple maternity dress of forest-green that was as no-nonsense as the queen's attire.

Her demeanor, however, was in no way no-nonsense. No, the woman was clearly agitated about something, and judging by the way her gaze darted anxiously from one person to another, obviously distressed to find so many people gathered in her mother's quarters.

"Princess Megan," Marcus whispered from his place beside Shane.

For a moment, Princess Megan only stood at the door, gripping it fiercely with one hand and looking panicky. Then, "Mother!" she shouted as she darted across the room toward the queen. "You must come quickly! Father has regained consciousness! He's coming out of his coma! He's going to be all right!"

Eleven

Shane sat in his room at the palace, feeling as morose as he'd ever felt in his life and wondering what the hell was going to happen now. And not where King Morgan was concerned, either, though, granted, he'd been as caught up as anyone in the commotion that had broken loose in the queen's quarters earlier that day. When Princess Megan had crashed the gathering with her news that the king was coming out of his coma, everybody in the room had jumped up and started clamoring incoherently, to the point where Shane hadn't known what any of them were saying.

Which hadn't seemed to matter, because after that, no one had seemed to be overly concerned with his presence anymore anyway. Queen Marissa had graciously excused herself and told Shane they'd talk later, then she and the members of the RET to whom he had been introduced had fled behind the princess. He and Marcus had been left alone, and retreated to the guest room assigned to Shane to catch up on all that had happened. In the interim, they'd received a report from Princess Megan that the king was fully conscious, but still a bit disoriented. The royal physician, however, was predicting that His Majesty would make a full recovery, though it would be a long process. And, unfortunately, the princess had added sadly, King Morgan wasn't going to be in a fit state to rule his kingdom, and would have to quickly make a decision about his predecessor. With that in mind, she had told the brothers that the DNA testing had been scheduled for the following day.

Surprisingly, however, their possible future as kings of Penwyck hadn't been what Shane and Marcus had spent the afternoon talking about. No, they'd been far more concerned with far more important matters: namely, the women in their lives.

"You have to tell her," Marcus said now from where he stood beside the window. "You have to tell Sara how you feel."

He was dressed in the suit he'd worn earlier, as was Shane. But where Marcus's was still faultless and businesslike, Shane's had pretty much decomposed. His tie hung unfettered from his collar, and the top two buttons of his shirt were unfastened. His jacket and trousers looked crumpled and unkempt, and he marveled at how Marcus was able to maintain the unsullied comportment that totally eluded Shane. In spite of what the queen had said earlier about their resemblance to each other, few people would ever have taken them to be brothers, let alone twins. But then, that was one of the great things about their relationship—they loved each other in spite of their many differences.

"But tell her what?" Shane asked. "I don't know how I feel."

Marcus smiled. "The hell you don't."

"I don't," he insisted.

Marcus sighed. "Four letters. One syllable. Rhymes with shove. Which is what I'm going to do to you if you don't admit how you feel."

Shane swallowed with some difficulty. "But how do I know I...love her? I mean, maybe it was just the circumstances, you know? Maybe it was one of those things where two people are thrown together in an extreme situation, and they just naturally sort of turn to each other because there's no one else. How can I know for sure if it's love?"

Marcus's smile grew broader. But all he offered in response was "Oh, you know."

Shane opened his mouth to object, then closed it again. Because in that moment, deep down, he did know. He knew that Sara was unlike any woman he'd ever met in his life, and he also knew that the way he'd responded to her was completely different from the way he'd ever responded to a woman in his life. And he'd started to respond that way long before the hijacking had occurred. Long before they'd been taken hostage and thrown into dire straits. He'd responded the minute he met her. And that response had only grown with every word they'd exchanged and every moment they'd shared. Maybe it had happened more quickly because of their circumstances, but even if everything had gone the way it was supposed to, he'd still feel this way about Sara. He *knew* that. He knew it. He'd still want to be with her now, more than he wanted to be anywhere else.

So why wasn't he with her?

"I can ask Amira for her address," Marcus said, seemingly reading his mind. "She'll know where to find Sara."

Shane glanced down at his watch. It wasn't even dinnertime yet. Maybe if he left now, he and Sara could go out somewhere and talk. Or better yet, stay in and talk. He didn't care. As long as they could talk. As long as they were together. As long as they could stay that way for the rest of their lives.

He nodded to Marcus. "Yeah. I'd like to see her. Talk to her. Thanks, bro," he said. "I owe you."

Marcus shook his head. "You owe Amira. And she'll only ask that you don't make an obnoxious toast to the bride and groom at our wedding."

Shane laughed. "It's a deal. But only if you return the favor at my wedding."

Sara was just coming down the stairs into the main entry of her mother's house when she heard a car pull up out front. Goodness, Devon and his parents were already here, and her mother wasn't dressed yet—she'd have to greet them herself. Drat early birds, she thought. And drat this dress, she thought further, halting in front of the mirror at the foot of the sweeping circular staircase to haul up the bodice that kept threatening to fall dangerously low. And drat the designer, too. Obviously he'd been thinking wishfully about the average woman's bust line when he'd conceived it.

And while she was at it, drat all dinner parties, Sara further complained to herself. She'd forgotten all about her mother's having arranged this impromptu one with friends for Sara's brief, and unexpected, trip home. She'd tried to get her mother to cancel it—considering everything Sara had been through over the last couple of days, entertaining guests was the last thing she wanted to do—but her mother had been adamant. It would only be five other people, her mother had reminded her. Unfortunately, that five included one Devon Trent, an old schoolmate of Sara's whom her mother still insisted would make a suitable husband for her daughter.

It was more important now than ever that they have the little soiree, her mother had insisted, because now they could celebrate her safe return from those dastardly kidnappers, as well. It would bolster Sara's spirits after her unfortunate experiences.

Unfortunate experiences, she thought again as she struggled with the strapless, pale blue silk gown. She only wished those experiences all *had* been unfortunate. But no matter how badly she might recall some of the events of the past few days, Sara could never truly think of them as unfortunate. Because they'd given her her time with Shane, however brief it had been. And also because they'd offered her an opportunity to grow and change, for the better. She'd learned a lot about herself over the past several days. And she'd known, for the first time in her life, what it was like to be in love.

Because no matter how much she had tried to deny it since waking that morning beside Shane, Sara knew without question that she had fallen in love with him. She wasn't sure when or how it had happened, only that it had. Pragmatic, sensible Sara Wallington had fallen head over heels in love at first sight.

No, not first sight, she quickly corrected herself. Oh, she'd been very much attracted to Shane from the start, but it had only been when she'd witnessed his outgoing personality and his wry sense of humor, even in the face of danger, and noted his tenderness and sweetness that she had started to have feelings for him. And those feelings had come to fruition last night—though, truly, it felt like ages ago now—when the two of them made love.

She was in love with Shane Cordello. Even though she knew he wasn't the kind of man who would stay around for long.

But don't cry, Sara, she told herself. *Oh, certainly you'll think back on this time with wistfulness and yearning. But life goes on. So much to do. You'll have your career. Probably. Once Admiral Monteque forgives you for botching the first assignment you ever received and bumps you up from the RII mail room, where you're bound to start your career—if you start at all. Why, in fifty years or so, you might even make it up to the steno pool.*

She sighed heavily and surveyed her image in the mirror one last time. She'd dressed formally, as her mother always dictated for such affairs. Above the costly blue silk gown, a diamond choker encircled her neck, and coupled with it were diamond earrings and a matching bracelet around her white-gloved wrist. Her pale red hair was wound up into a sleek French twist, and she'd done her best with her cosmetics to hide the shadows beneath her eyes.

The doorbell rang again, so she turned and hurried to answer it.

"Devon, you impatient boy," she said as she pulled the door open...only to find Shane Cordello standing on the other side.

He looked tired and rumpled, and utterly incongruous in a dark suit and tie. Well, perhaps not *too* incongruous, she decided upon further inspection. The tie, after all, was knotted inexpertly, and the shirt was misbuttoned and the entire ensemble appeared to have been slept in. He looked wholly uncomfortable in the formal clothing where he'd been so at ease in his ragged jeans. She couldn't help smiling at the picture he presented now, as if he were wearing his big brother's clothes and not quite pulling off the image he wanted. Could it be that he was trying to impress her? she wondered. Why had he come here tonight?

"Who the hell is Devon?" he asked by way of a greeting. "And why the hell would he be impatient?"

She noticed then that Shane wasn't smiling, but looked sullen and irritated instead. And was that petulance she heard in his voice when he was asking her about another man? How very intriguing...

"Hello, Shane," she said, amazed that she was able to keep her voice level. "It's good to see you again, too."

His dark brows arrowed downward. "I mean it, dammit. Who the hell is Devon?" He turned his attention to her attire then, and his features went slack. "Holy cow. You look gorgeous. You look like..."

"What?"

He smiled, but there was nothing happy in the gesture at all. "You look like a princess," he said sadly, though why such a thing would make him unhappy, Sara couldn't have said. "Am I interrupting something?"

"Yes," she told him. "You've interrupted what was promising to be a very dull evening. Do come in, please."

She could scarcely believe he was here. She really hadn't expected to see him again, ever. She'd been told by the RII that his time in Penwyck had been scheduled down to the last minute, and that if the DNA tests on him and his brother came back positive, then his entire life would be scheduled down to the last minute, too. What had been left for Sara to deduce—which she had, smart woman that she was—was that those minutes would not include anyone outside the palace or the royal family. Certainly not the woman who had botched his delivery to Penwyck in the first place.

She had allowed herself to hope that he might telephone her when he had a chance, but she'd entertained no false dreams there. No matter what had passed between the two of them, Shane Cordello wasn't the kind of man to run after a woman. Especially a woman he hadn't known long. Especially a woman to whom he'd made no promises.

But he had run after her, she realized now. He was standing right there in her mother's foyer, his gaze… Well. His gaze wasn't exactly fixed on her anymore. No, it was wandering over the foyer, up the long circular stairway behind her and into the rooms that flanked the entry—the grand salon to the right, and the massive music room to the left. She couldn't imagine what he must be thinking.

"Nice house," he said.

Oh. That was what he'd been thinking.

"I mean, *really* nice house," he reiterated. "Reminds me of the palace. Only…bigger."

"Not really," Sara said. "They're roughly the same size."

"Ah."

"Well, originally, the palace in Marlestone was only meant to be the royal family's summer home. This, of course, has been my family's permanent home for three hundred years now."

"Ah."

And with that one quietly uttered sound, for some reason, he seemed to go from angry to thoroughly demoralized.

"Shane?" Sara asked. "Is there something wrong?"

He took in her attire again, his focus lingering on the necklace circling her throat. He lifted his hand to the diamonds, running the pad of his index finger lightly, slowly, over each of the sparkling gems. Sara closed her eyes, willing him to drop his hand lower, to touch the bare skin of her throat and neck and shoulders instead. But he drew his hand back again before doing so, leaving her feeling bereft and cheated and gloomy. When she opened her eyes, it was to see him trailing his gaze around the sumptuous furnishings of the house again. So she followed his gaze, trying to look at her surroundings with an outsider's eye, only realizing then how very lush and ornate—and excessively overdone—the place was. Really, her mother should donate many of the pieces and artwork to the Royal Museum. They were only gathering dust—and appreciating to frightful amounts of value—here at home.

"Shane?" she said, turning her attention to him again.

"You, uh… You grew up here, I guess, huh?"

She nodded.

"You must like living this way."

"I never really thought much about it, to be honest."

"No, I suppose not," he said. "I guess you'd take this for granted."

"Well, I wouldn't say that, either."

He was still standing framed in the doorway, had scarcely taken two steps inside the house, and was looking as if he intended to turn around and leave again. So Sara did the only thing she could think to do. She reached for him, gripping him by both lapels, pulled him inside, slammed the door behind him pushed him back against it, and…

And kissed him for all she was worth.

Normally, Sara would never have been so forward. But then, normally, she wasn't in love with a man she had been terrified she would never see again. So she figured her behavior could be excused this once.

It evidently didn't bother Shane, though, because he responded by immediately roping his arms around her waist and pulling her hard against himself and fairly devouring her, too. For long moments, all they did was enjoy the embrace, neither of them speaking, only becoming reacquainted in the most fundamental way they knew how. Shane kissed her as if it had been months since he last saw her, and Sara reveled in his obvious desire for her, because it so mirrored hers for him.

"So does this mean you missed me?" Shane asked between kisses.

"Yes, desperately," she replied as she groped for breath and coherent thought.

He kissed her again. Then, "But it's only been hours since we saw each other," he pointed out.

"And it's been hell," she said, pressing her mouth to his once more.

"You're right," he agreed. "Hell."

Neither spoke for long moments after that, only embraced more heartily and kissed more passionately and clung to each other as if they never wanted to release the other again. Somehow, though, Sara registered the sound of another car pulling up outside, of two car doors opening and slamming shut, and she sprang away from Shane—but only far enough to stop the onslaught of his kisses, and temporarily at that.

"We need to talk," she said.

"Among other things," he assured her.

She smiled. "My mother's expecting guests."

"Yeah, this impatient Devon, for one. You never did tell me who he is or why he's impatient."

She grinned. "Jealous?"

"You're damned right I'm jealous."

"You have no need to be. There's no one but you, Shane."

His expression changed then, to one that told her how very relieved he was to hear her say such a thing. Honestly. Could he have ever doubted? she wondered. Could he have truly thought she would ever want anyone but him? Silly boy…

"Come upstairs," she said.

And without awaiting a reply, she took him by the hand and fairly dragged him up to her bedroom. She knocked on her mother's door as she passed, muttered something about lying down because she had a frightful headache and would be down to greet their guests in half an hour. She heard Shane chuckle and promise her it was going to last a hell of a lot longer than thirty minutes. Sara made a mental note to hold him to it. But first she wanted to hold him to herself. And no sooner had her bedroom door closed behind them than she pulled him into her arms and kissed him. Deeply. Wantonly. Needfully.

He wasted no time with words and went right into action, cupping her jaw with one hand to urge her mouth open wider for the penetration of his tongue. Then he easily pushed the top of her gown down to her waist, baring her breasts—what a brilliant man the designer was to have foreseen such a need for the garment, she thought vaguely—and filled his hand with one of the tender globes. Impatiently, he palmed her, rubbing her breast in intimate circles, kneading the delicate flesh in impetuous fingers. Then he tore his mouth away from hers and kissed her throat, her neck, her shoulder, before lowering his head to draw the erect peak of her breast deep into his mouth.

She tangled her fingers in his dark hair as he began to suck at her, pushing his head, his mouth, more firmly against her. "I—I thought we were going to…to talk," she gasped.

"Haven't you heard?" he said, the words coming warm and damp against her skin. "Actions speak louder than words. And right now, I'm pretty much shouting at the top of my lungs."

So he was, Sara thought. So he was. So what could she do but listen to him? Listen and contribute her own side of the conversation.

For long moments he tugged at her breast, mouthing the taut, sensitive peak, sliding the tip of his tongue along its lower curve. When he straightened to kiss her again, she reached for his tie, pulling the length of silk free from his collar to cast it aside. His jacket went next, when she skimmed her hands beneath it and pushed it off his shoulders, and she hastily went to work on the buttons of his shirt. That garment, too, was then cast aside, and Sara made immediately for his belt and the zipper on his trousers.

And never in her life had she felt so comfortable and correct as she did in that moment, undressing a man. Because it wasn't just any man she was undressing. No, it was the man she wanted. The man she needed. The man she loved.

He found the zipper at the side of her dress and yanked it down in concert with her opening of his own trousers, then pushed at the pale blue silk until it slipped down over her hips, pooling in a soft puddle at her feet. And then she stood before him wearing only white silk panties she had donned over white silk stockings with garters, and pale blue satin high heels. Shane groaned when he saw her attire, and her fingers on his trousers stilled.

"Oh, man," he said. "Do you realize how many men fantasize about seeing a woman dressed this way?" Then a thought seemed to occur to him. "Why are you dressed this way? I didn't think women wore garter belts anymore, unless they were anticipating…"

Sara smiled a seductive little smile. "They do if they think it feels erotic under their clothing," she said.

Shane gaped softly at her. "Are you telling me…"

"I always wear braces, Shane. Garters to you," she said, translating the term to American. "They make me feel—" she smiled naughtily "—like a woman," she finally finished. "Just because I wasn't sexually active before doesn't mean I never felt sexual, you know."

"Oh, man," he muttered again. "So then the whole time we were together up there on the mountain, you were wearing…"

"Well, not the entire time. I had to slip out of them when I took off my shirt to make bandages. My stockings were a mess."

"But before that?"

"Yes, I was wearing them before that."

He shook his head in disbelief. "Oh, man. If I'd known…"

"Yes?" she asked with much interest.

This time he was the one to smile naughtily. "We could have had a real interesting time in the washroom on the jet, Sara. And you wouldn't have been able to put a stop to it that night on the mountain, either."

"And tonight?" she asked.

His smile went positively wicked at that. "I don't think you want to call a stop to it tonight."

"Damn. Am I that transparent?"

He took advantage of her question to give her a thorough once-over from head to toe. "Um, in case you didn't notice, sweetheart, you're more than transparent. You're almost naked."

Though he quickly went about rectifying that, hooking his thumbs in her panties and pulling them down over her hips. Sara aided him the rest of the way, until all she had left on were her braces and heels. She started to removed those, too, but Shane halted her with a gentle hand.

"Keep them on," he said roughly. "I like you that way."

"Nearly naked?" she asked.

"All the best parts are naked," he assured her.

She sighed fretfully, throwing a wistful look at his loosened—but not yet removed—trousers. "Yet you defy nudity yourself. Spoilsport."

He pulled her against him, her naked breasts rubbing intimately against his bare chest, stirring parts of her that she hadn't thought could be any more stirred. "You want me naked?" he asked.

"Oh, yes, please," she told him.

"Then go for it."

She needed no further encouragement. Gripping the waistband of his trousers in back, Sara began to push them down with his briefs, over his taut buttocks, his trim hips, his lean thighs, kneeling before him as she pulled them down around his ankles, until he could step out of the garments and she could toss them to the side. As she began to rise slowly again, her cheek brushed the rigid member between his legs, standing now at full attention, and, impulsively, she dropped a swift kiss along its length. Shane caught his breath at the gesture, and when she understood why, she turned her head and slid the tip of her tongue along its full length, then parted her lips to draw him fully inside.

"Oh, Sara..." he said as she gripped his thighs and moved her head forward, taking as much of him into her mouth as she could. He uttered another sound, too, one that was feral and wild and uncontrolled, and she reveled in this newly discovered power she held over him. For long moments, she pleasured him orally, loving the way he twined his fingers in her hair to urge her gently forward even more. She only stopped when she felt his fingers gripping her shoulders, silently encouraging her to stand. But he said nothing as he met her gaze and grinned a drunken grin. Still, she was fairly certain she knew what he was thinking.

Slowly, wordlessly, he began to walk her backward toward her bed, but he surprised her yet again when they got there. Instead of waiting for her to turn down the coverlet, when she turned around and bent to perform the action, he stepped up and, without warning, covered her hips with his hands and entered her deeply from behind. Sara gasped at his entry and tried to straighten, but he opened one hand over the small of her back, and gently he bent over again. His other hand dipped beneath her, catching her breast and giving it a tempered squeeze.

Obediently, she bent forward, gripping the side of the bed and spreading her legs wider. Shane moved his hands back to her hips then and pulled her body toward his, deepening his penetration even more. He skimmed the pad of his thumb lightly up and down the length of the silky garter pressing into her buttock, then moved his digit to the center of her bottom, caressing her, creasing her, pressing lightly into her. Sara caught her breath at the intimacy, pushing her hips back more, taking him deeper inside her.

Again and again he entered her that way, the friction of him inside her delicious in a way Sara could never have imagined. But just when she thought she would spiral completely out of control, he withdrew, turning her around to face him, kissing her deeply again.

And as he kissed her, he urged her back onto the bed. Sara lay back with her legs dangling over the side of the mattress, and Shane stepped forward to enter her again. He jerked her legs up and hooked her ankles around his waist, then thrust into her, closing his eyes at the sensations that must have been winding through him. Sensations, Sara guessed, that were much like the ones she felt herself. She threw her arms up over her head and let the ripples wash over her, glorying in the rapid pace of his thrusting, knowing it was she who held him in such thrall, giving herself over to him just as completely.

With one final hard plunge, Shane threw back his head and cried out his culmination, and mere seconds afterward, Sara followed him, fairly melting under the onslaught. For one long moment, it felt almost as if time had stood still, absorbing them into one perfect, consummate, eternal climax. And then that moment ebbed, and she slowly returned to earth. Shane collapsed onto the bed beside her, and somehow, between the two of them, they managed to pull back the coverlet and crawl beneath it. There, they clung to each other, holding fast, as if each feared letting the other go.

For long moments, they only lay silent, catching their breath, gathering their thoughts. Then, softly, Sara said, "Well, I suppose I should take you downstairs and introduce you to my mother."

Beside her, Shane chuckled. "I'd rather meet this Devon guy. You never did tell me who the hell he is."

"He's the man my mother would like me to marry."

Shane stopped chuckling at that. "Then, by all means," he said, "introduce me to your mother. And Devon, too, the schmuck. Think they'd notice if I didn't bother putting on my pants?"

"Well, it would certainly make a statement, wouldn't it?"

"Damned straight."

Sara waited to see if he would say specifically what that statement might be, but nothing more was forthcoming. So she only snuggled more closely against him and wished with all her heart that he would be able to see how very much she loved him without her having to put voice to the words, because she simply wasn't sure she could say them just yet.

Instead, he changed the subject, though he didn't seem all that eager to do it. "I guess you heard about King Morgan?" he asked softly as he held her close, his voice sounding troubled and uncertain.

She nodded. "Word travels fast in Penwyck, you know. It's a wonderful relief to realize that His Majesty is going to be all right."

"Not able to rule anymore, though," Shane pointed out.

"No," Sara agreed. "But at least Broderick will have to step down now. Did you know it's been rumored that he himself is the head of the bloody Black Knights?"

This was obviously news to Shane, because when she glanced up to gauge his reaction, his dark brows had shot right up into his hair.

"There's not been any proof, mind you," she added. "But there are those who think he's been calling the shots over the years. Me included, frankly. There's just too much gone unanswered for it not to be him."

"So what happens if they find out that's true?" Shane asked.

"I imagine the RET will have much to say about it. At least he's been forced down now and won't be in line to rule the kingdom."

"But King Morgan *will* have to name his successor," Shane said.

Sara sensed the anxiety in his voice when he spoke. "You're afraid they're right, and that you and your brother might be the missing heirs."

He nodded. "I keep telling myself it's impossible. That there's no way I could be…of royal blood," he finished in a melodramatic tone. "But as long as there's a chance…"

"What will you do if you and Marcus *are* the missing heirs?"

"I don't know," he said. "I really don't know."

Sara wished she knew what to say that might soothe his worries, but she could only watch in silence as he let the thoughts tumble through his brain. Finally, though, he looked down and met her gaze levelly. "There's one thing I do know, though," he told her.

"What?" she asked.

He hesitated a moment, then, very softly, he said, "I know I want you to be with me no matter what."

She smiled. "Of course I'll be with you when you find out the truth, Shane. That's what friends are for."

He shook his head. "That's not what I meant. I want you to be with me when I find out the truth, sure. But, Sara…"

"What?" she asked, suddenly feeling breathless for no reason she could name.

"I want you to be with me after that, too," he said. "I want…"

"What?"

"I want you to be with me…forever."

Oh, dear heavens…

"And not as my friend. Well, not just my friend," he hastily qualified.

She narrowed her eyes at him, still afraid to let herself hope. "What do mean?"

"I mean…" He sighed fitfully. "Look, do you think you could see yourself spending your life with a guy who's not noble?"

She smiled. "You're noble, Shane. Whether or not you're a prince has nothing to do with that."

"But I mean… Could you be with a man who's just a regular guy?"

She shook her head. "No, I'm afraid not."

He looked stricken by her response. "You couldn't?"

"No," she said again. "Look, I'm sorry. But I'd rather have someone like you."

Now he looked confused. "What…?"

Sara laughed, certain now that they were both on the same wavelength, even if Shane was still at sea. "I don't want a regular guy, Shane. I want a special one. I want you."

He seemed to think about that for a minute, then, very slowly, he began to smile. "Oh. Okay." Then he turned grave again. "But what if I end up being king?"

"Then you'll be a special guy who wears a crown to formal functions," she told him. She rose up on her elbows, wanting to meet him eye to eye when she said what she had to say. "I don't care *what* you *do,* Shane, whether you're ruling a country or hammering a nail into a piece of wood. I care about *who* you *are.* And who you are is…" She smiled. "Extraordinary."

He grinned, obviously relieved. "Is that all?"

"No," she told him. "You're also the man I love."

He reached up to cup her cheek in his palm, his eyes filled with longing and promise and love and…so much more. "I love you, too, Sara," he told her solemnly. "So whattaya say? Will you marry me?"

"And be your queen?" she asked with a smile.

He nodded. "Not that my kingdom comes to much," he said. "I'm reasonably certain I've lost my job at the construction site, and chances are slim that I'm going to be the once and future king here in Penwyck. So, really, my domain is pretty much a one-bedroom rented condo in Malibu, and a vintage Jeep Cherokee. Oh, I do have a really bitchin' Yater surfboard, though. There are people in high places who would *kill* to own that."

Sara laughed. "I'll make protecting it my first assignment when I go to work for the California Security System."

Shane arrowed his dark brows down in concern. "I thought you had a job waiting at the RII. Which, now that I think about it, will mean you have a helluva commute to work every morning if you agree to be my queen and co-monarch."

She shook her head. "I think I can safely say that my future at the RII has been compromised before I even started there. Besides, after the grilling and skewering I got this afternoon about our Black Knights adventure, I think I can safely say I have no desire to work for the RII anyway. I'd much rather accept the job I was offered earlier this year by one of my professor's former students. She's a high-ranking official with the CSS, and she needs someone to work in the L.A. office whose specialty is counterterrorism, which, what do you know, just so happens to be the focus of my studies."

"Well, my, my, my. Isn't that convenient?" Shane asked.

"Yes, isn't it?"

"So you'll be the queen of counterterrorists, and I'll be the king of the unemployment line."

Sara laughed harder. "Sounds like a match made in heaven."

"Or, at the very least," Shane said, "a match made in Penwyck." He pulled her close again, and lifted his head to cover her mouth with his. "I love you, Sara Wallington," he said as he pulled away. "No matter who or what you turn out to be."

"And I love you, Shane Cordello," she readily replied. "No matter who or what you turn out to be."

And as they drew together for a kiss to seal the bargain, they both knew that *that* was really the only thing that mattered.

*　*　*　*　*

Who is the real royal heir?
Find out in next month's
CROWN & GLORY, *grand finale,*
ROYALLY PREGNANT
by Barbara McCauley

presents

A brand-new miniseries about the Connellys of Chicago,
a wealthy, powerful American family tied by blood to the
royal family of the island kingdom of Altaria.
They're wealthy, powerful and rocked by
scandal, betrayal...and passion!

Look for a whole year of glamorous and
utterly romantic tales in 2002:

Where love comes alive™

If you enjoyed what you just read,
then we've got an offer you can't resist!

Take 2 bestselling love stories FREE!

Plus get a FREE surprise gift!

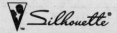

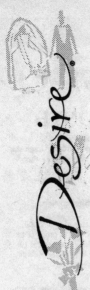

October 2002
TAMING THE OUTLAW
#1465 by Cindy Gerard

Don't miss bestselling author
Cindy Gerard's exciting story about
a sexy cowboy's reunion with his
old flame—and the daughter he
didn't know he had!

November 2002
ALL IN THE GAME
#1471 by Barbara Boswell

In the latest tale by beloved
Desire author Barbara Boswell,
a feisty beauty joins her twin as a
reality game show contestant in an
island paradise...and comes face-to-
face with her teenage crush!

December 2002
A COWBOY & A GENTLEMAN
#1477 by Ann Major

Sparks fly when two fiery Texans are
brought together by matchmaking
relatives, in this dynamic story by
the ever-popular Ann Major.

MAN OF THE MONTH

Some men are made for lovin'—and you're sure to love
these three upcoming men of the month!

Available at your favorite retail outlet.

COMING NEXT MONTH

#1477 A COWBOY & A GENTLEMAN—Ann Major
Zoe Duke ran off to Greece to nurse her broken heart, and the last person she expected to come face-to-face with was her high school sweetheart—the irresistible Anthony. He had made love to and then betrayed her eight years before. But he was back, and though he still made her feverish with desire, could she trust him?

#1478 CHEROKEE MARRIAGE DARE—Sheri WhiteFeather
Dynasties: The Connellys
Never one to resist a challenge, feisty Maggie Connelly vowed to save tall, dark and brooding Luke Starwind's soul. In exchange, he had to promise to marry her—if she could rescue him from his demons. Maggie ached for Luke, and while he seemed determined to keep his distance from her, *she* was determined to break him down—one kiss at a time….

#1479 A YOUNGER MAN—Rochelle Alers
Veronica Johnson-Hamlin had escaped to her vacation home for some much-needed rest and relaxation. When her car got a flat tire, J. Kumi Walker, a gorgeous ex-marine ten years her junior, came to her aid. Veronica quickly discovered how much she and Kumi had in common—including a sizzling attraction. But would family problems and their age difference keep them apart?

#1480 ROYALLY PREGNANT—Barbara McCauley
Crown and Glory
Forced to do the bidding of terrorists in exchange for her grandmother's life, Emily Bridgewater staged an accident, faked amnesia and set out to seduce Prince Dylan Penwyck. But Emily hadn't counted on falling for her handsome target. Dylan was everything she wanted…and the father of her unborn child. She only hoped he would forgive her once he learned the truth.

#1481 HER TEXAN TEMPTATION—Shirley Rogers
Upon her father's death, Mary Beth Adams returned to Texas to take over her family's ranch. She would do anything to keep the ranch—even accept help from cowboy Deke McCall, the man she'd always secretly loved. There was an undeniable attraction between them, but Mary Beth wanted more than just Deke's body—she wanted his heart!

#1482 BABY & THE BEAST—Laura Wright
When millionaire recluse Michael Wulf rescued a very pregnant Isabella Spencer from a blizzard, he didn't expect to have to deliver her baby, Emily. Days passed, and Michael's frozen heart began to thaw in response to lovely Isabella's hot kisses. Michael yearned to be a part of Isabella's life, but could he let go of the past and embrace the love of a lifetime?

SDCNM1102